FISHY BUSINESS

ROBERT LEE

Rock Salmon, an experienced private investigator, and his faithful pilotfish, Sanderson, find themselves involved up to their gills in gangland warfare when they meet the luscious Angel Sweetlips in Rock's office in downtown *Atlantis*.

Who has stolen the Sacred Chank, the rarest shell in the ocean? Is it Enzo Barracuda, the mob chief, or the elusive and slippery Ed Stingray? Rock and Hercule Poisson, the Intergill police inspector, join forces with Barracuda as the picture changes – there is more at stake than small fry when the clues lead straight to the arch villain, the rival gangland chief, Ernst Fishfinger.

ROBERT LEE

Fishy Business

Illustrated by Caroline Holden

A Magnet Book

First published in Great Britain 1981
by Methuen Children's Books Ltd
Magnet edition first published 1982
by Methuen Children's Books Ltd
11 New Fetter Lane, London EC4P 4EE
Copyright © 1981 Robert Lee
Illustrations copyright © 1981 Methuen Children's Books Ltd
Printed in Great Britain by
Cox & Wyman Ltd, Reading

ISBN 0 416 24820 9

Contents

To two oranges and a lemon

The cast in order of appearance

Rock Salmon	*A Private Fish*
Sanderson	*His Discreet Assistant*
Angel Sweetlips	*A Dame*
Otto Grass	*A Prawnbroker*
The Hatchet Fish	*Villainous Bodyguards to the Mobs*
Hammerhead	*A (lovable) villain*
Enzo Barracuda	*The Mob Chief*
Hercule Poisson	*An Inspector of Police at Intergill*
Turtleneck	*A Book-keeper*
Ed Stingray	*A Nasty Piece of Work*
Red Snapper	*A Newspaper Reporter/ Photographer*

Police Constable Dover	*A Flat Fish*
Cuckoo Major	*A Dolphin*
Bluehop	*A Dolphin*
Hai Leap	*The Dolphins' Guru — also a dolphin*
The Dolphin Patrol	
Fishfinger	*The Arch Villain*
His Army of Great Whites, led by Layla Blue	*A Slinky Blue Shark*
Fargo	*An Albatross*
Count Orca	*A Killer Whale*
Mary, Duchess of India	*Orca's Wife*
Carlos	*A Portuguese Man of War*
Carlos	*"*
Carlos	*"*
Carlos	*"*

Countless Fish of all shapes and sizes, from sea-horses to sharks. . . .

1 · Introducing Mr Salmon

Rock Salmon felt uneasy. There were no two ways about it. Swimming towards the old quarter of town, he had plenty of time to think about the events of the past hour. It took quite a lot to rattle an experienced dogfish like Rock, but the unexpected entrance of Angel Sweetlips into his office in downtown Atlantis had sent danger signals rattling up and down his spine.

He had been trying to sleep off the night before. Sanderson, his faithful Pilotfish, was determined not to allow him to be disturbed. This was standard procedure on any morning after an enjoyable evening spent by Rock down in his favourite club – *Ronnie Scuba's Dive*. However on this particular morning Rock was rudely awakened by a fearful commotion in the outer office. Voices were being raised. Tempers were being lost.

'I haven't swum all this way to be told I can't

even see him,' spoke an excited female voice. 'I need a good private detective and I need one now!'

'Please, Miss,' replied Sanderson, 'I'm sure Mr Salmon will be only too happy to help you, but I have been given strict instructions not to disturb him, as it were, for the next two hours.'

'But I have to see him now,' was the reply. And with that the owner of the female voice burst into Rock's office, hotly pursued by a somewhat flustered Sanderson.

'Awfully sorry about this, sir,' said Sanderson. 'A highly persistent customer, as it were.'

'Okay, Sanderson,' replied Rock. 'I can see you did your best.'

'Mr Salmon?' asked the excited intruder, 'Mr Rock Salmon?'

'The same,' replied Rock, who, despite the hour of the day was hardly able to take his eyes off her.

'At last,' she sighed. 'May I sit down?'

'Be my guest,' replied Rock, rather nervously.

'I suppose I ought to come straight to the point, Mr Salmon – or can I call you Rock?'

'Please do.'

'My name is Sweetlips,' she went on, 'Angel

Sweetlips. You may have heard of my guardian, Enzo Barracuda.'

Rock's heart skipped a beat, but he managed to maintain a cool expression. Barracuda was the undisputed gangland chief of Atlantis, with a strong hold on all underwater business enterprises.

'Sure, I've heard of him,' gulped Rock casually.

'Well,' she said, 'A few days ago – on my birthday to be precise – Enzo threw a party for me. It was just an excuse for him to show off my birthday present, I think. He's very vain, and the present was beautiful. Have you ever heard of the Sacred Chank, Rock?'

'No,' replied Rock. 'I can't say I have.'

'The Sacred Chank is a shell, but not just an ordinary shell. It is the rarest shell in the ocean. And it's surrounded by fabulous stories, half history and half legend.'

'Very impressive,' noted Rock.

'To cut a long story short, Rock,' sighed Angel, 'I seem to have lost it.'

'Stolen?' asked Rock.

'I suppose it must have been,' answered Angel. 'It can't have just vanished.'

'Then why not tell Barracuda?' suggested

Rock. 'You can be sure his hoods will find the wretched thing just as quickly as I can.'

'That's the whole point,' said Angel. 'I don't want him to know that it's gone. If you can trace it for me, there may be a chance that we can get it back before anyone is any the wiser.'

Rock was still unable to take his eyes off her. Just his type, he thought. Come to think of it she was most guys' type. She was the sort of fish that brought out the protective instincts in a guy. Rock knew instinctively that he was letting himself in for all sorts of danger by wanting to help, but he couldn't resist her. After all, he reasoned to himself, I'm a normal cold-blooded fish.

'Oh, Rock,' pleaded Angel, 'you will help me, won't you? No one else will, not even Errol Fynn.'

'Not even Fynn, huh?' replied Rock, not in the least offended that Angel should have gone to Fynn before trying him. 'Okay, babe, you're on.'

'Oh, thank you, Rock,' she cried. 'I knew I could count on you. Of course I'll pay all your expenses. Money's no object. This is for starters.'

She handed him a thick wad which Rock

didn't even bother to count. He put it straight into his desk drawer.

'Now tell me, Miss Sweetlips . . .'

'Oh, please call me Angel,' she interrupted.

'Okay,' continued Rock. 'Tell me, Angel, did you know everyone at your birthday party? Or was there anyone you think might have been capable of stealing the Chank?'

'There was only one fish there that I didn't know, but he seemed friendly.'

'Can you remember his name?' asked Rock.

13

'Yes, I can,' said Angel thoughtfully. 'His name was Stingray, Ed Stingray.'

'Okay,' said Rock. 'He's quite possibly in the clear, but at least he's a lead. We'll start enquiries right away.'

'And will you come round to my place tomorrow evening so that I can tell you all about the Sacred Chank? Nine o'clock? The address is 2212 Marine Avenue on the corner of Marine and Lagoon. You can't miss it.'

'I'll be there at nine,' replied Rock as Angel swam out swishing her tail.

'Holy fish!' exclaimed Rock, under his bubbles.

As the door shut behind her, Sanderson swam in. He was an inconspicuous little chap and though cheerful by nature he always looked slightly worried about something.

'Well, Sanderson,' said Rock, 'I presume you listened in to that cosy little chat. What do you reckon?'

'If you don't mind me saying so, sir,' said Sanderson, 'you may well be getting yourself into deep water, as it were.'

'I know, Sanderson, I know,' replied Rock. 'And I appreciate your concern. But you must admit – that's quite a lady, eh?'

'Well, sir, it's not always wise to mix business with pleasure, if you follow my drift.'

'Sure I follow your drift, little fellow,' replied Rock. 'But come on, enough talk. We've got work to do. I want you to check out the Shellfish crowd and find out anything you can about Stingray. I'm going to snoop around the old quarter of town.'

And so it was an uneasy Rock Salmon who arrived in the Old Quarter of town and swam through the warrens of tiny streets full of quaint old shops buried in the mouths of hidden caves.

Rock headed for one particular shop, tucked away in a small row of jewellers and trinket shops known as Haddock Gardens. He stopped outside. There hung the familiar sign of the Prawnbrokers Guild. Inside, through the frosted windows, shone a dim light. A bell tinkled over the door as he swam into the musky old place. The shop was full of the usual bric-à-brac, but at the far end there were two unusual carved cases containing beautiful pearl necklaces and gorgeous coral earrings and expensive-looking fin watches. Rock was wishing that he could afford to buy such classy stuff, when the

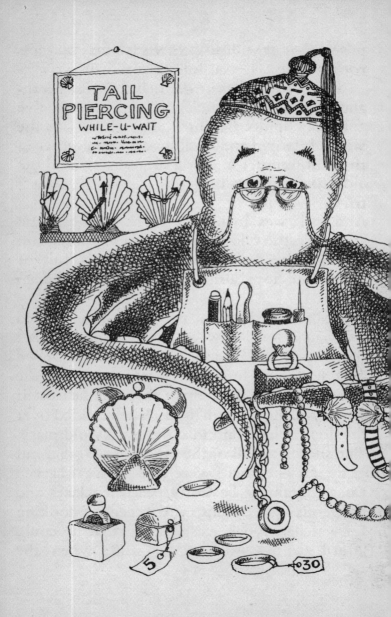

proprietor of the shop slithered in from the back room.

'Hello, Rock – long time no see,' spoke an old and high-pitched voice.

Rock studied the lined face of Otto Grass, whose bright eyes were twinkling behind gold-rimmed spectacles.

'Hello, Otto, you old sucker,' he said. 'How's tricks?'

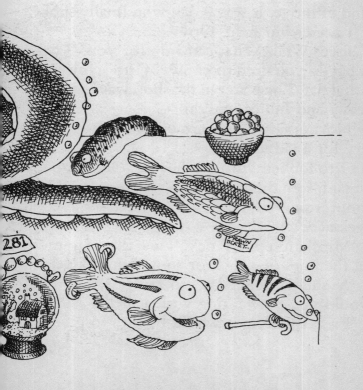

There was very little happening in the ocean that Otto Grass didn't know about. He made sure that he kept a watchful tentacle on every-day life in Atlantis. Although he had the appearance of a kindly old man, Otto was never quite to be trusted.

'Oh, you know,' replied Otto, 'can't complain, can't complain.'

There was a silence. The two fish seemed both to be waiting for the other to make some kind of move. It was Rock who finally spoke:

'I need your help, Otto.'

'I see. Well. What can I do for you, Rock? What do you need to know?' Otto's voice was rather flat. The water in the shop was somehow heavy and full of tension.

'No, no, Otto, I want to buy a piece of jewellery for a lady friend.'

Otto looked visibly relieved. 'Good, good,' he said, sounding a little more cheerful. 'How about some nice pearls? Or maybe a coral necklace?'

'Mm,' muttered Rock. 'I was thinking more on the lines of a shell or something like that.'

'A shell?' replied Otto, surprised. 'What would you be wanting with a shell?'

'I was thinking it would be nice to give her

something romantic, something with a touch of history behind it.' Rock looked straight into Otto's eyes. 'How about a Sacred Chank, Otto?'

Otto didn't bat an eyelid. 'I don't think that's a very good idea, my friend. Out of your price range, I fear. I don't happen to have a Sacred Chank in stock. Now, if you'll excuse me, I'm rather busy.'

Suddenly Otto was moving his several limbs in different directions around the shop, closing up display cases and drawing shutters.

'I thought it was too good to be true,' he muttered. 'You wouldn't swim all the way from your end of town to Haddock Gardens just to buy a present for a lady friend. Not you. And you know very well that you are swimming into very murky waters. Forget the Sacred Chank, Rock. Listen to the words of an old Octopus. Forget it. It can bring you nothing but disaster.'

'Come on, Otto, you know me,' replied Rock. 'Disaster's my middle name.' He could see that Otto was looking extremely anxious.

'Otto,' he asked, 'have you ever heard the name Ed Stingray?'

'Please, Rock,' replied Otto, gravely. 'There

are certain questions one does not ask, just as there are certain fish one does not cross.'

'I see,' said Rock. 'You mean you're frightened of the mobs?'

'There are mobs and there are mobs, Rock,' replied Otto. 'Now, come on. Will you leave me in peace? Do you want to give an old man a heart attack? I can't talk. I think I've made my point.'

OTTO GRASS.

PRAWNBROKER

'Then you *have* heard of Stingray?' Ro͟ persisted.

'Go away, go away!' cried Otto, his voice growing higher and higher. 'No more questions.' And with that he sidled slickly into the back room and slammed the door.

2 · The Mobs

Rock felt that Otto had given him some kind of clue. Obviously another mob was involved, but Otto hadn't told him enough to really put his fin on it. The old man was too scared to talk. Rock decided to leave.

He swam out of the shop wondering what he should do next. His question was soon answered for him. He had company: Hatchet Fish — six of them. Horrible thin ghost-like creatures. Small fish with bulging eyes. Bad news.

'Are you gonna come peaceful?' spoke a nasty rasping voice in his ear. 'We don't want no trouble.'

Rock owed his survival in the seas of life more to his brain power than his muscle. This was no secret.

'Sure,' he replied. 'How can I refuse such a charming invitation?' A Hatchet prodded him in the ribs.

'Where are we going?' asked Rock.

'Just swim,' came the sharp reply. The Hatchets closed round him tightly as they swam through the back streets and alleys of the old Quarter of Atlantis.

Soon they were up in the business end of town. They were greeted by a hive of activity among the strange tower-blocks and office buildings. Small fish were darting in and out with briefcases and bowler hats and worried expressions on their faces. They were all in such a hurry that no one noticed Rock and his bodyguard slip quietly into the depths of the vast Transatlantic Building. Everyone was too busy minding their own business. Ironic, thought Rock. When you want people to mind their own business, they never do.

Up went Rock and the Hatchets to the very

top of the building. Down a long dark passage-way to a huge door. A Hatchet knocked on this and it seemed to open automatically and on they swam down another long dark passage-way until they came to another door. This one swung open without the Hatchets even knocking, and with it came a great shaft of sun-light through the water which seemed to make its own way back down the passageway. Rock relaxed a little and swam through into the warmth of the sunlight.

Suddenly he froze. He was confronted by a huge shark. A Hammerhead, with a weather-beaten face and beady eyes and a polkadot bow-tie.

'It's us, Hammerhead,' screeched one of the Hatchets.

'Good work, lads,' replied Hammerhead. Soon Rock was being bundled through yet another door and into a large white office.

'Hammerhead,' spoke a cool smooth voice. 'You seem to have had a stunning effect on our guest. Would you pour him a drink?'

Rock was aware that he was in the presence of Barracuda himself and he no longer felt quite so terrified. They were obviously not out to do him harm. Barracuda just wanted to talk.

The drink seemed to revive him and he was able to take in his surroundings. There was an uncanny stillness in the water. Enzo Barracuda was not a huge fish. Hammerhead was far bigger. But there was something about Barracuda that inspired a feeling of respect. The neatness of the jawline, the long scar down the right

cheek, the way his monocle seemed to magnify one side of his face; Rock wasn't sure what it was. He put it down to sheer presence. Hammerhead was at his side. Huge but almost kindly in comparison. The epitome of the gentle giant.

As Rock sipped at his drink he began to feel better.

'I'm sorry to have given you such a shock, Mr Salmon,' said Barracuda. Hammerhead laughed, a big bellow of a laugh.

'Cor, guv',' he said, 'you should have seen yourself in a mirror. You looked as though you'd been filleted.' This started him laughing again. Rock was not amused, but he didn't say anything.

'And now, quickly to business,' said Barracuda briskly. 'My people tell me that my ward Angel Sweetlips has paid you a visit, Mr Salmon.' There hardly seemed any point in Rock's denying it, so he didn't.

'She probably wants you to recover the Sacred Chank for her. Am I right?' Barracuda continued.

'Yes,' replied Rock. 'Quite correct.' He was surprised. Barracuda seemed to know everything, as though it had all been planned.

'You don't have to worry on her behalf, Mr

Salmon,' said Barracuda. 'I fully understand her excellent motives in coming to you. Quite honourable. However it will be unnecessary for you to involve yourself any further in the matter. Everything is firmly under control. And this is a private affair. Do I make myself quite clear, Mr Salmon?'

Barracuda looked straight into Rock's eyes. He felt a shiver go up his spine. He decided that he'd definitely caught the drift of Barracuda's message.

'You don't have to worry on my account, Mr Barracuda,' he replied meekly.

'Good,' replied Barracuda with a smile. 'I'm delighted to meet such a reasonable fish. All that you need to do as far as Angel is concerned is to make some excuse in order to relieve yourself from the case. I feel obliged to pay you for your no doubt valuable time. Hammerhead, will you see to it? Good day, Mr Salmon. My Hatchets will escort you back.'

'Don't worry, I'll find my own way out,' said Rock, and the meeting was at an end. Hammerhead handed him a wad of money as he was leaving, and Rock swam straight back to his own office. He felt as tired as a fish out of water.

3 · An Unofficial Mission

When Rock arrived back in his office he was greeted by the law; an official-looking fish nosing through his files.

'*Bonjour*, Rock. How are you, *mon ami*?' It was Chief Inspector Hercule Poisson of Intergill – the ocean's far-reaching police force.

'I'm fine, thanks, Inspector,' replied Rock. 'How are my private papers?'

'Please do not take offence, *Monsieur*. I just want to know if there is anything that you know that I do not about a certain character.'

'His name?' asked Rock, who was in no mood to beat about the seaweed.

'Stingray,' replied Poisson.

What a popular fish this Ed Stingray was becoming, thought Rock to himself. 'Why do you ask, Inspector?' he inquired.

'I ask you for your own good,' replied

Poisson. 'You are becoming involved in an enormous conspiracy.' Rock didn't reply.

'Ed Stingray,' persisted Poisson. 'You know him?'

'We've never met,' replied Rock truthfully.

'But have you heard of him, Rock?'

'I have, Inspector.' It was the small voice of Sanderson. He had a way of appearing out of nowhere. Uncanny.

'Sanderson,' interrupted Rock. 'I'd forgotten all about you. How are you? How did you get on? We may as well let the Inspector in on it all. We seem to be covering the same water, after all.'

'Well, Rock,' said Sanderson, 'I went down to the bottom to see the Shellfish crowd, as you suggested, and asked them questions about Ed Stingray and the Sacred Chank and they all shut up like clams.'

'I see,' said Rock. 'So then what did you do?'

'I consulted my old friend Turtleneck, the book-keeper at the race-track, and I discovered that there's something very fishy going on in tomorrow's big race. Large bets have been put on two outsiders by none other than Ed Stingray. He must have got the race rigged in some way, sir, as it were.'

'Very interesting,' mumbled Poisson. 'Very interesting.'

'We've got to do something!' exclaimed Rock.

'I have a little plan, sir, which I think will upset Mr Stingray's,' said Sanderson.

'Will anyone get hurt?' asked Poisson.

'No, Inspector. At least I hope not,' replied Sanderson. 'My plan involves no violence.'

'*Bon*,' said Poisson. 'You must proceed then, Sanderson. I will have some of my undercover fish there just in case.'

'But why all the big fuss suddenly about this petty crook Stingray?' demanded Rock.

'Because of Fishfinger,' replied Poisson.

'Fishfinger?'

'Ernst Fishfinger,' said Poisson. 'If my information is correct, this Fishfinger and his gang intend to muscle in on the mobs here and take over the entire city, bit by bit. Now we all know that the Barracuda mob are a fairly heavy bunch, if you know what I mean. But at least we know that there is some kind of balance in the city. Not so the Fishfinger mob. Do you remember the South Sea Bank Job?'

'Yeah,' said Rock. 'Wasn't that the one where no clues were left at all, just a load of dead fish?'

'Correct, *mon brave*. And they got away with half a million guilders.' Rock whistled. Poisson continued. 'The South Sea Bank Job was only one among several similar capers, all of them unsolved, all of them with the same trademark – no clues. Fishfinger is a real mystery. We know very little about him, he is virtually a recluse, we don't even know what he looks like. But we do know that he has a passion for beauty, and is one of the ocean's biggest collectors of rare objects and antiques.'

'Of course,' interrupted Rock, 'the Sacred Chank. Barracuda must have been aware that it could prove an interesting lead from Stingray to Fishfinger. Fascinating.'

'What is your plan then, Sanderson?' asked Poisson.

'Just to make sure that Stingray's horses don't win the race, Inspector,' replied Sanderson. 'You can be sure he'll be using Fishfinger's money.'

'But no doping of the horses, eh?' warned Poisson.

'No, of course not. That's not sporting, is it?'

'Then I will leave you now, *mes amis*,' said Poisson. '*Au revoir*, until tomorrow.'

'Goodbye, Inspector,' said Rock. 'Keep your gills crossed.'

'I think I'll turn in early tonight, sir,' said Sanderson, after the Inspector had left. 'Tomorrow's a big day.'

Rock was relaxing in his easy chair, idly going through the latest edition of *Playfish*. 'Goodnight, Sanderson,' he said drowsily. 'Sleep well.'

Within ten minutes they were both sound asleep. Rock dreamed vividly that night of dolphins and sharks and of a huge killer whale. Was it a premonition?

4 · The Race

The crowds were out in force at Coral Stadium when Rock arrived, and the first and second races had been ridden and won. The layout of the course was simple: a huge circuit of water was neatly marked out by white parallel fences. At one point in the track it divided into two. One track continued round so that it formed a big circle. The other branched off into the distance before curving back and joining the original track. This diversion was only used for long-distance races, and the race that Rock had come to see was to be run on the short, circular course. Rock swam through the thick crowd of fish to his place in the Grandstand. Sanderson had swum off to prepare his plan. Rock had time to take in his surroundings. In front of him, down by the white rails that fenced off the crowd from the track, he could see the touts with that strange bubble code that they always used. He decided to swim down to see for himself what bets the punters were making.

'Fancy a small flutter, mate?' asked a bookie as Rock swam past him.

'No thanks, not today,' replied Rock.

'Very wise, Mr Salmon, sir, very wise.' And with that, the bookie gave Rock a huge wink.

Of course, thought Rock. This must be Turtleneck, Sanderson's friend. At this point he was rudely and suddenly brushed aside by a stingray.

'I want all this on Mermaid and Davy Jones, each way,' said the stingray.

'Okay, guv',' said Turtleneck, 'You're on.'

Rock thought it best not to hang around. He guessed that this was none other than Ed Stingray, and he did not want Turtleneck to mention his own name again in front of him. At the moment Stingray had probably never heard of him. Rock winked at Turtleneck and slipped back into the crowd and so to his place in the Grandstand.

He watched the seahorses swim slowly along to the starting gate, some of them chatting to each other, some of them remaining nervously silent. He looked around him. At the back of the Grandstand were the important fish, sitting in their smart boxes. Rock noticed Poisson in one of these with a couple of other fish. Then further down there was Hammerhead, towering over his boss Enzo Barracuda who was looking thoughtfully through the race guide. Rock wondered whether he knew that Stingray was up to no good. And where was Stingray?

Rock's question was soon answered, for at that moment a smug-looking Ed Stingray swam into the box next to Barracuda's. He even had the nerve to peer over into Barracuda's box. Goodness, thought Rock, I'd like to listen in on that conversation. And what if Barracuda intends to deal with Stingray right here at the races?

No, surely not, thought Rock. Barracuda's after Fishfinger, not Stingray. He's just small fry. Rock had no more time to brood as just then a voice boomed over the public address system: 'They're under starters' orders ... and they're off.' The crowd roared as twenty seahorses hopped out of the starting traps and scooted nimbly off round the course. So far there was no sign of Sanderson.

The seahorses were swimming fast. At first they all stuck together, but soon there were

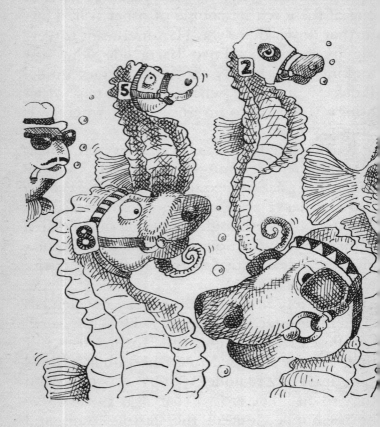

only three making the running: **Davy Jones in the lead followed by Mermaid and third, Seaweed.** The rest of the field were slow by comparison. As they came up to the first fence,

36

Rock began to worry. Still no sign of Sanderson. Mermaid and Davy Jones were neck and
neck at the first. The commentator's voice was
full of excitement as they took the jump. They

37

sprang nimbly onto the fence, twirled their tails round it in a loop and spun themselves off at great speed. The crowd roared. A classic hurdle. Seaweed followed in hot pursuit. The first three horses were breaking away from the field. One horse managed to flick himself off the jump in the wrong direction. He was clearly out of the race.

Rock glanced behind him. Ed Stingray was still looking as smug as ever, and Hammerhead was out of his seat. It was obvious that he and Barracuda had backed Seaweed to win.

Now two leaders were swimming ahead boldly. Over they went. The second fence was cleared perfectly, and the third. Seaweed was beginning to tire. Two more fences to go. Surely nothing could stop the leaders now? Through his binoculars Rock thought he saw them exchange sidelong grins at each other. The commentator's voice over the public address system seemed to have shot up an octave as he grew more and more excited. Ed Stingray was sniggering to himself. Barracuda and Hammerhead looked grim.

The two leaders jumped over the second from last fence with great ease. They were approaching the point on the course where it divided. One fence to go and a quick sprint to the finish. Seaweed was battling bravely on, ahead of the rest of the field. Rock watched the leaders again through his binoculars. The crowd by now were up on their tails, in a fever of excitement. Then Rock noticed the expression on Mermaid's face change from confidence to panic, and he was looking back at the field in horror and disbelief. What was happening? Rock looked ahead of them. About fifty yards in front of the leaders was another seahorse. Yes, there was no mistaking it. And moving well. No wonder the two horses looked so horrified. They were no longer in the lead.

Mermaid looked at Davy Jones as if to say, 'Right, come on, we'll show him, whoever he is,' and took off in pursuit. Even faster. On and on they went, with only one thought, to get ahead of this threat to their victory.

Rock couldn't believe what was happening. The seahorse in the lead was deliberately taking them off onto the long–distance track. Of course! It was Sanderson in disguise. Rock cheered and cheered. The two horses were in such a panic to catch up that they took the bait. They were narrowing the gap. And then it began to dawn on them that the last fence hadn't arrived. Worse, it wasn't even ahead of them. They looked behind anxiously and too late they realised they had been tricked. No horses behind them. They looked ahead: the mystery seahorse had vanished.

The crowd was in a turmoil. The commentator was shrieking now at the top of his voice: 'And there they go now. The two leaders have gone completely off their heads and onto the wrong part of the course. And now, yes, it's Seaweed. It's Seaweed all the way. What a race. Nothing can stop him now. And as they come over the finishing line it's Seaweed the winner.'

Rock was aghast. Of course he realised that it could only have been Sanderson who had side-tracked the leaders, but he was none the less stunned. What a brilliant plan. He turned round. Poisson, Hammerhead and Barracuda were all jumping up and down in great excitement, and Ed Stingray was just sitting there furious.

'Well, sir,' puffed a small voice beside Rock. 'I think I gave them a swim for their money, as it were.'

'Sanderson,' beamed Rock, 'You're a genius.'

'Thank you, sir,' he replied. 'You couldn't give me a lift back, could you? I'm a bit puffed.'

'Hop aboard, Sanderson,' grinned Rock.

The crowd was beginning to settle down again, except of course for the fish who had succeeded in backing the winner. They were all making their way down to the bookie area to collect their winnings. The water was warm, the late afternoon sun reflecting on the roof of the Grandstand. Rock thought that maybe he ought to have a quick word with Poisson, but Sanderson was almost asleep on his back. Better take the little fellow home, he decided.

As he turned away he was aware of a piercing noise in the water. Someone had fired a gun. There was a commotion going on round Barracuda's box. The crowd were stampeding away from the smart area. Panic in the water. And blood.

'What is it? What's going on?' he asked a fish swimming away frantically.

'Someone's taken a pot-shot at Enzo Barracuda,' the fish replied before scurrying off.

'Oh, no,' muttered Rock. *Where was Stingray?* he thought.

'Look, sir, quickly,' cried Sanderson, as though reading his mind. And sure enough, there was Stingray, swimming fast, losing himself in the general hysteria.

41

'Holy fish,' said Rock. 'Maybe we should get out of here, and fast.'

'I agree, sir,' said Sanderson. 'There's nothing we can do that Hammerhead and Poisson between them can't, if you see what I mean.'

'Precisely,' said Rock. Sanderson hung on tightly to the fin on Rock's back and they swam quickly homewards.

5 · The Dolphin Patrol

The Press managed to arrive at Rock's office before he did. An excited Red Snapper was questioning Rock before he'd even reached the door.

'Is it true, Mr Salmon, that you have recently had dealings with Enzo Barracuda? Are you in any way involved with the attempt on his life?'

'Attempt?' asked Rock. 'Do you mean Barracuda is not dead?'

'Yeah,' replied Snapper. 'Didn't you know? Only a flesh wound. Got him in the dorsal. He's gonna be all right.'

'Holy fish, that's a relief,' sighed Rock. 'Did they manage to catch Stingray?'

'No, he got clean away. But wait a minute, I'm meant to be asking the questions, not you.'

'Not now, Red,' said Rock. 'I'm not in the mood.'

'Oh, come on, Mr Salmon. Give a poor fish a break.'

'No go, Red.' And with that, Rock managed to close the door between himself and the frustrated reporter.

Sanderson was sound asleep, so Rock put him quietly to bed and then nestled back into his own easy chair. It was good to put his tail up at last. He thought that he heard the 'phone ringing, but the sound came from miles away and he decided to ignore it. Finally the noise grew louder and louder. Rock opened his eyes. The 'phone was ringing through the water, loud and clear. Sanderson was still fast asleep. It was morning. Rock staggered over to the receiver.

'Hello,' he mumbled. 'Oh, yes, Inspector. Sure, I'll be right over.' He put the phone down.

'The good Inspector Poisson would like to see us, I suppose,' spoke a little voice. Rock turned round and smiled.

'Good morning, Sanderson. I didn't want to wake you.'

'Oh, that's quite all right, sir. I suspect that today's going to be somewhat hectic, as it were.'

'Come on, then,' said Rock. 'I presume that you want to come with me to Intergill.'

'Let's go,' said Sanderson.

And off they went.

Poisson was not in his office when Rock and Sanderson arrived at Intergill Headquarters, but Rock was expected. A flat-fish who introduced himself as Police Constable Dover invited Rock to proceed with him to the roof. P.C. Dover didn't notice Sanderson, who was travelling discreetly in the shadow of Rock's fins.

Rock swam up to the roof of Intergill. Dolphins were undergoing a special kind of Physical Education programme.

'Glad you could make it, *mon ami*,' whispered Poisson.

'What's the low-down on Enzo Barracuda, Inspector?'

'Oh, no problem,' replied Poisson. 'He's going to be okay. And word has it that he wants to reward you and Sanderson for the way you dealt with Stingray's horses.'

'Well that's a relief,' said Rock.

'I thought you'd be interested to see the Dolphin Patrol's Frip Fu class,' said Poisson, changing the subject.

'What Wu?' mumbled Rock.

'No, Rock. Frip Fu. The ancient dolphin art of self defence and unflippered combat.' Rock turned and watched.

Two dolphins faced one another and bowed with inscrutable half-smiles on their faces, then with two complete somersaults in the water, they crashed into each other belly to belly with a force that Rock could feel from where he was standing. One of them managed to hook the other over his back and send him flying through the water. They both swam fast to the surface, disappeared for a moment, and then crashed back in without ever losing those inscrutable smiles.

'Blavo, blavo,' cheered an old dolphin with a lined face and wise eyes. He was obviously the dolphins' guru. 'Vely good, Cuckoo. An excerent attack.' The two dolphins bowed humbly before their master, who bowed back at them, slowly clapping his flippers.

'That's Hai Leap,' whispered Poisson, 'The authority on Frip Fu. Rumour has it that he's even taken on a killer whale and lived to tell the tale.'

'And who are the two dolphins that were fighting?' asked Rock.

'Cuckoo Major – he's in charge of the patrol – and his friend Bluehop,' said Poisson. 'And here they come now.'

After Poisson had carried out the formal introductions, Cuckoo asked why he had omitted to introduce Rock's small travelling companion. Poisson looked at Sanderson in amazement.

'*Mon dieu*,' he said. 'I hope you will forgive

my bad manners, Monsieur Sanderson. I really did not see you down there.'

'Quite all right, Inspector,' replied Sanderson. 'Actually I was travelling incognito, as it were.'

Rock was impressed by the sharpness of Cuckoo's eye. He would definitely be an extremely good guy to have on the home team.

'Okay, my friends, now listen to me.' Poisson spoke as though he were bringing a meeting to order. 'It is vital that we have a rendez-vous with Enzo Barracuda as soon as possible. I have made overtures and he is not unwilling to talk to us. He is quite aware of the threat.'

'You mean the threat of Ed Stingray?' asked Rock.

'I mean Fishfinger,' said Poisson gravely.

There was silence in the water. Somehow the threat of Fishfinger was far more terrible than that of Stingray. At least they all knew what Stingray looked like, arrogant sneer and all. But Fishfinger. There was something dark and evil about him. An evil that the imagination magnified a hundred times. The water seemed suddenly cold. They all felt it.

'Well, Inspector,' Cuckoo Major broke the silence. 'Unless there's anything else, I think we'll get on with our training.'

'Oh, but of course,' said the Inspector.

'See you soon, Cuckoo,' said Rock. Cuckoo winked back and with a flip in his tail swam into formation with the other dolphins, hotly pursued by his friend Bluehop.

'Well, Inspector, that was interesting,' said Rock. 'And now I have another appointment. The dame. We might get some leads out of her. I mean we've still got no idea where Fishfinger's mob operates from. I've got a feeling that Miss Angel Sweetlips might be able to help us with our enquiries.'

'I wish you luck, Rock,' said Poisson.

'Thank you, Inspector. I think I'll need it.'

6 · Over at Angel's

Rock took Sanderson with him to Angel's place. The little chap was so inconspicuous that he was virtually invisible, and Rock hoped that Angel might provide them at least with a clue.

Marine Avenue is the chic suburb of Atlantis, where all the smart fish live. A beautiful view of the mountains and comparatively un-polluted waters was the setting for Angel Sweetlips' residence. It was one of those strange mixtures of styles that would have stuck out like a sore fin in any other city in the sea, but here in Atlantis it did not seem even mildly objectionable or obtrusive.

Rock and Sanderson were swimming up the drive nervously when there was a huge vibra-tion in the water. Instinct told Rock to take cover behind the nearest clump of coral, and as he did so, the front door of the house burst open and out flew Ed Stingray in a terrible rage. He encircled the house once in a great arc and swam off into the night.

'Wow, Sanderson, that was a close one.' No reply. 'Sanderson? Hey, come on, where are you?' There was no sign of him. Maybe he'd got caught up in the rush of Stingray's exit. He wouldn't have survived that, thought Rock. No way. Or maybe he'd managed to attach himself to Stingray as he tore past him. The odds against that must be huge, thought Rock, as he approached the front door with trepidation. He knocked and there was no answer. The door was open so he swam in, unannounced.

Angel was in tears on the sofa, a large bruise down the side of her face. She was wearing a dress of sheer net, but this was not the time to think about such things.

'Hey, babe, come on,' said Rock, as he poured them both a drink. He sat next to her and stroked her back sympathetically. She looked up at him.

'Oh, Rock,' she sobbed, 'I'm so glad you're here. I just don't understand, I don't understand.' She's not the only one, thought Rock.

The drink seemed to calm Angel down a little, and Rock felt the time had come for an explanation.

'Angel,' he said, 'just tell me exactly what's been going on.'

'I lied to you about something when I came to see you, Rock. I didn't think it was important.' She broke into floods of tears all over again.

'Hey, it's okay,' said Rock. 'I can guess. Stingray's your boyfriend and you didn't want anyone to know. That's okay.'

'How did you know?' she asked, pulling herself together again.

'I didn't until just now,' replied Rock. 'It was a calculated guess.'

'Well,' continued Angel, 'you know it all now. Enzo, my guardian doesn't know. He would probably kill me if he did. After the incident at the races I wanted to call the whole thing off with Ed. And also there's the Sacred Chank. I'm sure he's got it. But I can't prove it. When he came here this evening and I told him I wasn't going to see him any more, he went off his head, smashed me across the face and left in a temper.' She got up and swam around the room.

'Rock,' she said, 'you're so calm and patient. I like you.'

'Yeah?' said Rock, and if he hadn't been a fish he would have blushed. 'You ain't too bad yourself.'

'You have the kind of face that looks as though you've been through it all and back again,' she said. She was looking straight into Rock's eye. Their gills were moving slowly now, in time. The water felt breathless.

Not now, thought Rock. There's work to do. Is she telling the truth, this dame? Can she be trusted?

His thoughts were quickly answered. The water in the room was suddenly a swirl of bubbles and Rock felt a crashing blow that knocked him sideways. He just had time to see the blurred face of Ed Stingray staring down at him angrily before he lost consciousness and sank into a whirlpool of black water.

7 · The Godfish

Rock woke up in strange surroundings. He knew for sure that he was in hot water. He was in a tiny cell and his head was swimming. He was not alone. 'Hello there, Mr Salmon. Nice to have some company, at last.' It was the reporter, Red Snapper.

'Where are we?' asked Rock, 'and what are you doing here?'

'Big Reef,' replied Red Snapper. 'Seems like I got a little too close to the mark in the story I was doing on one Ernst Fishfinger. I got clobbered as I was leaving your office.'

'You mean we're in Fishfinger's hideout?' exclaimed Rock.

'Not so much a hideout, more like a terrorist camp,' said Red. 'Wait till you see the layout of this place.'

Rock couldn't help wondering why he had been brought all the way to Big Reef. Surely if Fishfinger and Stingray wanted him out of the way it would have been easier just to kill him. No. Fishfinger must need him for something. Rock was on the point of asking Red some questions about the camp when the door opened and some Hatchets came in.

'Take me to your leader,' replied Rock with a sarcastic flourish.

'Best of luck, Mr Salmon,' said Red Snapper as the cell door slammed shut.

They didn't swim out into open water. The cell seemed to be part of a man-wreck. Every now and then while travelling the oceans a fish can experience the sight of one of these sad remnants of Man's efforts to negotiate the sea. The wreck which housed Rock's prison cell had, like most man-wrecks, a depressing atmosphere. A smell of death. Rock felt uneasy. The Hatchets led him through the body of the ship to what must have been one of the staterooms, a large and at one time luxurious cabin. The man-wreck must have been an ocean liner in her day and the sharks must have feasted for a week when she went down.

Rock swam slowly into the stateroom of the

huge dead liner and was quickly aware of the presence of the Big Fish himself. He looked around.

'Ah, Mr Rock Salmon, so good of you to come.' Rock focused his eyes on the speaker of these honied words. Ernst Fishfinger himself. Rock's gills started to function irregularly.

It wasn't that Fishfinger was particularly long. He wasn't. It was the sheer bulk of him. He seemed to be massively bloated and out of proportion. His voice was sickly and syrupy. He oozed insincerity. Rock looked coldly into his bulging eyes and then shifted his gaze to the menacing fish on his left – Ed Stingray. What a sinister pair, thought Rock, looking at both of them, Fishfinger – fat and slippery and full of evil – and Stingray – who might have been good looking if his features had not been contorted into ugliness by the hate that he bore for fishkind. All of this went through Rock's head in a split second. It seemed an appropriate time to engage Fishfinger in conversation.

'Hello, Fatso,' he said, avoiding Stingray and looking straight at the fat fish. Ed Stingray completely lost his temper at this and hurled himself at Rock.

'I'll teach you to show respect to Mr

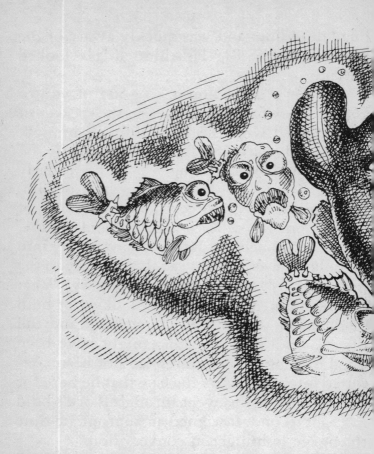

Fishfinger, you creep,' he bellowed. Rock easily sideswam him.

Fishfinger laughed. 'Calm yourself, Ed. Take it easy. So impulsive. After all, a rock can break your bones but a word can never hurt, isn't that

right, Mr Salmon?' And with that he looked straight into Rock's eyes with a look of utter disgust and chuckled. His whole body quivered like a jelly as he did so. Ed Stingray managed to take a grip on himself and slunk back, sulking.

As he did so, Rock's eyes almost popped out of his head. There, tucked beneath Stingray's stomach, were the small but unmistakable features of Sanderson. He winked at Rock. Rock managed not to reveal his secret to the others.

'Why have you brought me here?' he asked Fishfinger.

'You do seem to have got yourself into rather deep water for a small-time private fish, wouldn't you say so, Mr Salmon?' Rock did not reply.

Fishfinger continued. 'In the normal course of events you realise that by now you would be dead. However I have reason to believe that you have something which I want very badly. I refer of course to the Sacred Chank.'

Of course, thought Rock. He had forgotten all about the Sacred Chank, the shell that Angel Sweetlips had lost. But according to her, Stingray had it. Rock looked slowly at Stingray. Interesting, he thought. No register in his eyes at all. Then maybe Stingray didn't steal it. That meant that Angel Sweetlips had lied to him and wanted everyone to believe it had been stolen, or else someone else had really stolen it. Enzo Barracuda maybe? But why?

Rock didn't have time to think his thoughts through.

'Where is the Sacred Chank, Mr Salmon?' asked Fishfinger. Rock decided to bluff. After all, Fishfinger seemed desperate to have the Chank.

'The Sacred Chank is quite safe,' he replied. Nobody moved, except Fishfinger. He just reached over and picked up a strange object.

'Do you know what this is, Mr Salmon?' he asked.

'No idea,' replied Rock.

'It is a human invention. I found it on this ship. It is a turkish pipe. Here, come, Mr Salmon. Sit next to me and I will show you what to do. Don't worry it won't bite, which is more than I can say for my rash friend here.' Fishfinger seemed to be lacking in respect for Ed Stingray.

'The humans use this contraption as a form of relaxation, Mr Salmon,' continued Fishfinger. By now he was puffing away at a long tube. Odd bubbles were curling up through the water and there was a peculiar smell in the room.

'It's called tobacco,' said Fishfinger. 'Please try some. It may help you to relax. And believe

me, you had better relax, Mr Salmon. I want to know where the Sacred Chank is.'

'Sorry, Fatso, I don't want any of your tobacco. They say it damages your health. And I'm not talking.' Ed Stingray was up and ready to jump on Rock again, but Fishfinger held him back with one look.

'Perhaps I can persuade you to co-operate, Mr Salmon,' he said slowly. 'Come with me.'

With this, Fishfinger put down his pipe and swam slowly and awkwardly out of the state-room and up on to the open deck. From there, Ed Stingray rushed ahead, returning a few moments later with an escort of roller skates pulling a strange, disc-like contraption. Rock watched in amazement as Fishfinger clambered clumsily aboard.

'Please join me in my limousine, Mr Salmon.'

'No thanks, I'd rather swim,' replied Rock.

'Suit yourself,' said Fishfinger. 'But this is the only way to travel.' Off they went, Fishfinger in his strange disco-submarine drawn by skates, Rock and Stingray and some Hatchets following on. Rock noticed that Sanderson had some-how managed to attach himself to him.

They swam through some of the most

beautiful sea-scapes that Rock had ever seen. They quite took his bubbles away. Formations of rocks that hinted at familiar shapes and patterns which the sunlight changed with every minute flicker of the water. Shallow waters producing the most beautiful coral beds and the most beautiful fish: fish of all shapes and sizes. Colours that Rock had not even dreamed about. It was as though another dimension had been added, as if existence in Atlantis lacked the essential details of gaiety and pretty fish. And yet Rock knew it was all a façade. Behind the glitter of Big Reef and its lure of coral power lurked another kind of power, the evil force of a megalomaniac. Fishfinger.

As they made their way through the coral beds, fish stopped whatever they were doing, looked at Fishfinger and turned their backs. They were scared. Rock could almost see the fear scurrying down their spines. He noticed that they were swimming nearer and nearer the surface and had come into a vast clearing. Nothing but shingle on the sea bed. He could feel the waters humming but could see nothing because the entourage had closed in around him. Then suddenly the group disbanded and Rock saw something that he would never forget for the rest of his life. There, in the waters of Big Reef, was a regimented army of twenty Great White Sharks swimming in strict formation and at that moment undergoing strict training. It took a little while for this to sink in. Great Whites are terrifying beasts at the best of times but everyone knows that they are normally loners. But here were twenty of them swimming and working together. Rock looked again and noticed their leader – a slim and dusky blue shark, a girl.

'Squad, attention,' barked the girl, and twenty Great White Sharks jumped to attention, their grim faces turned attentively towards their leader. The fact that this mere slip of a fish was able to maintain control over the Great Whites had the effect of unnerving Rock even more.

'Squad, dismissed,' was her next order, and the sharks all swam sombrely away. The slinky blue shark swam towards Fishfinger. The skates were supporting him on his disc in mid-water, their tails flickering to help circulate the water.

'Nice work, Layla,' said Fishfinger in his most gluey voice.

'Yes,' said the girl matter-of-factly. 'I think they're almost ready.' She looked at Rock and then back at Fishfinger as though to ask who the stranger was.

'Oh, I'm so sorry, my dear, let me introduce you to this gentleman – Layla Blue, Rock Salmon.'

'Pleased to meet you, Layla,' said Rock softly, looking her straight in the eyes to see if there was any hint of attraction there. Rock needed all the friends he could get at this moment. He was unlucky. Layla did not even reply, but just looked at him coldly for a second and turned back to Fishfinger.

'Is it wise for him to see us working?' she asked.

'Don't worry, my dear, Mr Salmon is not a problem, are you Mr Salmon?'

'Who, little me?' replied Rock.

'You see, Mr Salmon, the sands of time have almost run out for your friends in Atlantis. Very soon the city will be mine. There is nothing that anyone can do to prevent this happening. I have the most powerful army in the sea.'

'What about Count Orca and his killer whales?' asked Rock.

'He disbanded long ago,' said Fishfinger. 'He's no threat to us.'

'Too bad,' said Rock.

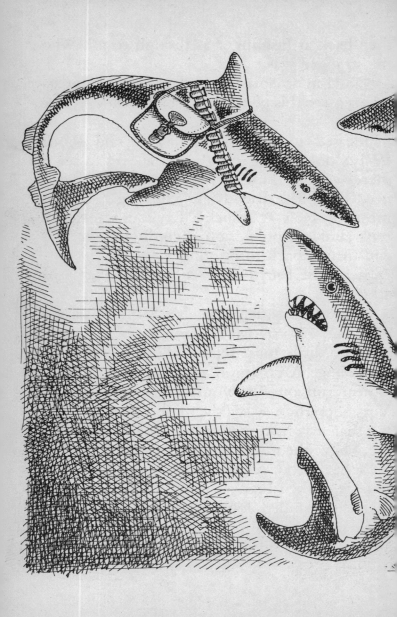

'You know that you do not need to suffer personally, Mr Salmon. You have something that I want. I will do a trade with you – the Sacred Chank for your life.'

'Mmm,' said Rock. 'I'll have to give it some thought.'

'Take your time, my friend. But bear it in mind that we march on Atlantis very soon!'

Rock's mind was racing. He knew that somehow or other he had to escape and warn Poisson and Barracuda. He was sure there must be some way to defend Atlantis.

'And now my Hatchets will escort you back to your quarters, Mr Salmon. Think hard, but above all come to the right decision. What is the point in being a dead hero?'

'If I tell you where the Chank is, will you call off the invasion?' asked Rock, suddenly. Fishfinger turned and faced him.

'Quite honestly, Mr Salmon, no. Not a chance. I intend to find the Sacred Chank with or without your help. Take him away.'

8 · Escape

Rock was taken back to his cell. Red Snapper looked relieved to see him.

'We've got to get out of here, Rock,' he said.

'No problem, a piece of hake, as it were,' said a small voice.

'Who's there? What's that?' asked Red in dismay, very jumpy. Rock laughed:

'Don't worry, Red, it's Sanderson. We'll be out of here in no time and on our way back to Atlantis.'

'Getting out is no problem, sir,' said Sanderson. 'It's staying out. They've got Mako sharks guarding the perimeter of the city. They've cast a net right round Big Reef. No one's allowed to leave.'

'Tricky, huh,' mumbled Rock. 'But at least we have the element of surprise on our side.'

'Leave it to me, sir,' said Sanderson. 'Do exactly as I say . . . if you don't object, that is?'

'Now is not the time for manners, Sanderson. Get on with it. Red doesn't mind, do you Red?'

'Not at all. You know, Sanderson, you're the nearest thing I've ever met to the Invisible Fish.'

Next time a Hatchet opened a grille in the cell door, Sanderson slipped out. Seconds later, the key was being tossed into the cell. Sanderson had done it!

'Come on,' he said, and there was a sense of urgency in his voice. 'I'll keep guard. We've got to get you out of here before the Hatchet gets back.' Rock had the door open in no time. He locked it again behind them, threw the key back inside and closed the grille. They swam out of the cell complex and into the open water, keeping very close to the coral buildings at the side of the street.

'This way,' whispered Sanderson. 'Come on, keep going.' On they swam, ducking as soon as anyone approached. They felt extremely conspicuous.

'We've got to find some disguises, Sanderson,' said Rock. 'Or else we'll never get out of here.'

'Follow me, sir,' replied Sanderson after a

72

moment's thought. They swam into the nearest cinema. A horror movie was showing – *The Fishmonger*. Very scary. Red managed to acquire some dark glasses from an unsuspecting cod who was too busy gulping at the horrors on the screen. Rock borrowed a hat off a dog-fish in the back row who was trying to kiss his girlfriend.

'Oh, come on, darling,' the dogfish was say-ing, 'just one little kiss.'

'Watch the film, Rover,' was her reply. She wasn't having any of it.

'How do we look, Sanderson?' asked Red as they left the cinema.

'Well ... different, sir, as it were.'

'Come on,' said Rock. 'No time to lose.' They swam off. This time they appeared to go unnoticed. They swam out through the suburbs of Big Reef, through the high-rise where all the Sardines lived huddled together in huge numbers, reeking of garlic and olive oil.

Soon they had reached the city limits. The Makos were at the checkpoints.

'Well, Sanderson,' said Rock, 'what now?'

'First of all we find a checkpoint where there's only one Mako on guard.'

They swam round the perimeter. It took about half an hour to find a suitable checkpoint. Only one guard was on duty.

'Right,' said Sanderson. 'Now listen to me.' Red Snapper and Rock huddled round to take in Sanderson's every word.

'I'm going to ask the guard whether he wants a clean-up. You know that's one of us Pilotfish's jobs. While I'm doing this, you both swim for it. And whatever you do you mustn't look back. Just swim as fast as you can.'

'That's the best plan you can come up with, Sanderson?' gulped Red.

'Can you think of anything better?' asked Rock. No one could, so they agreed to try. Sanderson swam off towards the Mako.

'Halt, who goes there?' shouted the Mako. What a sight: twelve feet of Mako met six inches of Sanderson nose to nose.

'It's only little me, guv',' said Sanderson. 'Just wondering if you were requiring a wash and brush up. Hmm . . .' he went on, swimming beneath the shark's stomach with the shark watching him all the time, 'this undercarriage hasn't been washed and waxed in years.' The Mako started to scratch his belly.

'You're right,' he rumbled.

75

'And look at this, sir,' said Sanderson, point-ing at the Mako's tail. Its eyes followed Sander-son down from the streamlined length of its body to its tip. Rock and Red counted one-two-three, took deep breaths and bolted as fast as they could.

Rock had swum about a hundred fins when he heard a heart-rending scream behind him in the water, followed by what felt like an explosion which sent him flying. He looked around. The Mako had taken Red in one bite and was coming after Rock. Nothing he could do. Rock's brain was racing. His only chance was at the bottom. He overtook poor Red's smashed dark glasses on the way down. He tried to hide in the shingle. He could hear the big brute swishing above him, excited by the taste of blood, trucking around, searching him out. *What has become of Sanderson?* thought Rock. He could feel the shark nosediving to-wards the sea bed, obviously on the right track. It was no use. He just had to accept it. This was the end.

He decided to make one last dash for it. He waited for the shark to nosedive the sea-bed again and then swam for his life. The waters were murky with the disturbed shingle but

Rock could just about see the sun shining through the water. And he could see a mackerel swimming slowly towards him. Not too deep.

'Look out! Look out!' screamed Rock as he tore past the Mackerel. By now the Mako had sensed that Rock was trying to make his get-away and had turned. Rock looked back and saw the great fish swimming straight towards him. He was scared out of his wits. The huge shark opened his jagged mouth and Rock waited. The Mako took the mackerel in one bite. *My turn now*, thought Rock as he closed his eyes. There was a sudden flurry of bubbles and the smell of panic in the water. As Rock opened his eyes he couldn't believe what he saw. The Mako had been hooked by a man-line. The mackerel was being used by humans as bait. No wonder the small fish did not try to get away. Rock looked up to the surface and saw what he hadn't noticed before – the unmistakable outline of a boat.

He didn't hang around and watch, just in case the Mako got away. He swam off as fast as he could and was soon joined by Sanderson. They were both silent for a while thinking about poor Red Snapper. So sudden and final; so unexpected.

77

'Sanderson,' said Rock finally. 'Get me back to Atlantis – and make it quick.'

'Right, sir.'

It took Rock and Sanderson two days before they finally arrived back home in Atlantis. There were no major incidents on the journey, except perhaps for one thing : they were swimming fairly near the surface above a rocky section of sea not far from land. The water was warm and both fish were tired. They'd been swimming non-stop for over a day. They were just idling along when the water above them burst open. Rock instinctively dived down. He was still very nervous after his near-miss with the Mako. He didn't know what to expect. But nothing happened. He looked up and saw a dark shape sitting on the surface. It was definitely not a fish.

'Looks like a bird, sir, as it were,' said Sanderson.

'We're safe enough from birds at any rate,' replied Rock.

As they spoke a strange thing happened. The bird put his head down under the water and said to them :

'Cuckoo must fetch Orca, Cuckoo must fetch Orca.'

'Who are you?' asked Rock.

'I am Fargo the Albatross,' replied the bird. 'Cuckoo must fetch Orca.'

'What do you mean? What for?' asked Rock.

'Fargo must go now,' said the bird, and flew away.

'Come back!' shouted Rock. But he knew that Fargo couldn't hear him. He would be up in the sky and flying away. *It must be strange to be out there*, thought Rock. *No water to support you. It must be very strange to be able to look down on the water.*

'Come on, sir, stop dreaming. We must not fall asleep. It's vital that we return. That Fargo bird always gives good advice. We must tell Cuckoo to fetch Orca.'

'Oh, you've met Fargo before, have you, Sanderson?' asked Rock.

'Not personally, sir, no,' replied Sanderson. 'But I know those who have – including our friend Inspector Poisson.'

'I wonder what Poisson is up to now,' mumbled Rock.

On and on they swam, until finally they reached Atlantis. They went straight up to the office. As they came in, Angel Sweetlips came out of the kitchen wearing a fishnet gown. When she saw that it was Rock she burst into tears.

'Oh, Rock, I've been so worried,' she cried.

'I think a nice cup of coffee would be in order,' said Sanderson, always the soul of discretion, and he disappeared into the kitchen.

Rock felt uneasy. Here he was back home at last, exhausted after a gruelling ordeal which had begun at the wrong end of a lead pipe, in this very lady's living room. He would have to be wary of Miss Angel Sweetlips. There was more to her than met the eye.

'How did you get in here, Angel?' he asked.

'The door was wide open,' she said. 'And everything was all over the place. Someone must have been looking for something. Your whole office had been turned right over. It's taken me ages to clear it all up.'

Rock looked around. Everything was tidy, but he noticed a few things out of their usual place.

'And what are you doing here, Angel?'

'I've been worried sick about you, Rock. What you must have thought. But I didn't betray you to Ed Stingray, I promise you.'

'I never said you did,' replied Rock cautiously. *What was all this about?* The last thing he needed now was an hysterical woman.

'Now why don't you run along and forget the whole thing?'

'But, Rock, you don't understand, I know who's got the Sacred Chank.' Rock looked at her keenly. She seemed quite grave and obviously concerned and worried. Despite himself Rock was inclined to think she was telling the truth.

'I think I know who's got it as well,' he replied. The Sacred Chank had certainly given Rock's nerves a run for their money. It would be good to get the wretched thing under lock and key and concentrate on the real dangers ahead.

'It seems then that we both know,' said Rock.

'This is no time for games, Rock. Hammerhead is looking after it for Enzo Barracuda.'

'Then we've nothing to worry about, have we?'

'Only that there are forces inside Atlantis who work for Ed Stingray who will stop at nothing to acquire the Chank.'

'I'll have a word with Barracuda and Hammerhead about it. We'll make sure it doesn't fall into the wrong fins.'

'Oh, Rock, I can't tell you what it means to me to see that you're okay,' said Angel. And with that she kissed him and swam out of the door before Rock had a chance to realise what had happened.

Sanderson came out of the kitchen and

whistled cheekily at Rock: '*Cherchez la femme,* eh, sir, as it were?'

'There's no time to lose, Sanderson,' replied Rock, dismissing Angel from his mind. 'You go over to Poisson. Get him and Cuckoo over to Enzo Barracuda's office as soon as you can. I'll meet you there.'

'Yes, sir, right away, sir,' said Sanderson.

Both fish swam off. They were absolutely exhausted but they had important work to do.

9 · The Longshot

Rock swam straight over to Barracuda's. It took a while for him to persuade the eel on the door that Hammerhead knew him.

Eventually Rock and Hammerhead were talking to the boss.

'We've just heard from Poisson, guv',' said Hammerhead. 'He's on his way over.'

'Good,' replied Rock. 'The sooner the better.'

Barracuda looked thinner than the last time Rock had seen him, but apart from that he seemed to show no outward signs of having been shot, at least from a distance.

'Please sit down, Rock,' said Enzo softly. 'Some coffee? You look as though you could do with a cup.'

'Thanks,' replied Rock.

'Mr Salmon, Mr Salmon. Wake up, guv'.'

'What, what?' muttered Rock. Somehow

Rock had managed to fall asleep soon after being offered coffee. Now he awoke with a start. Poisson, Sanderson and Cuckoo Major were all in the room.

'Monsieur Rock,' said Poisson, 'Sanderson has outlined to me briefly what has occurred and Monsieur Barracuda and I have decided to join forces to combat the threat from Fishfinger.'

'I'm very glad to hear that,' replied Rock, 'but there's something else that we need. You see, even the combined forces of Intergill and the mobs will not be enough to deal with Fishfinger's army. We have only one real chance.'

'And what is that?' asked Barracuda.

'Count Orca,' replied Rock.

You could have heard a jellyfish yawn, the silence was so electric. Poisson finally broke the silence.

'But, Rock, Orca is our sworn enemy.'

'Count Orca hates Fishfinger more then he hates us,' replied Cuckoo.

'Cuckoo,' said Rock, 'When Sanderson and I were swimming back from Big Reef we met an Albatross called Fargo. He kept saying, "Cuckoo must fetch Orca." I think the bird is right.'

'Yes, I think it might be possible,' said an

85

excited Poisson. 'You if anyone can do it, Cuckoo.'

There was silence again. Count Orca was that most terrifying of all sea creatures – a Killer Whale: a friend to Man but a friend to no fish. And Count Orca was King Killer Whale.

'What do you reckon, Cuckoo?' asked Hammerhead. 'Is it worth a go?'

'Well,' said Cuckoo cheerfully, 'we've certainly got nothing to lose.'

'I don't think we have much time,' said Rock. 'They must have realised that we got away. Chances are we've got twenty-four hours before the full invasion force arrives.'

'Cuckoo,' said Poisson, 'you go as fast as you can to Count Orca. Bluehop can be in command of the Patrol while you're gone.'

Hammerhead looked at Barracuda and Barracuda nodded.

'Inspector,' said Hammerhead gravely, 'me and the lads is at your disposal.'

'Only one condition, Inspector,' said Barracuda before Poisson could reply, 'complete amnesty for all prisoners when it's all over.'

'That's the least I can do, Monsieur,' replied Poisson with a smile. Cuckoo got up to leave.

'Give Bluehop a message from me, will you,

Inspector? Tell him to use man's net trick. Don't forget, now, will you?'

'I won't forget, Cuckoo,' replied Poisson.

'Good luck,' said Rock.

Cuckoo grinned at him. At this point, Rock fell into a deep sleep. He had quite forgotten to talk about the whereabouts of the Sacred Chank.

10 · Deep Sleep

In the depth of sleep Rock thought he could hear voices followed by the muffled sound of a door slamming. Suddenly he was alert. Someone was trying to attract his attention.

'Pst, Rock, it's me, Cuckoo Major.'

'Cuckoo – you! I thought you'd gone to fetch Count Orca,' said Rock in amazement.

'I want you to come with me,' replied Cuckoo.

'That's not the best joke I've ever heard, Cuckoo,' said Rock. 'I'm not too struck on the idea of ending up as the fish course of some whale's lunch.'

'You won't be, I can assure you,' said Cuckoo. 'But I'll have far more chance of arousing Orca's sympathy if you come with me. At least we can try to make it look like an official deputation from Atlantis.' Rock could see the logic behind Cuckoo's words.

'Okay,' he said, 'you've talked me into it. Let's go.'

The two headed out of Atlantis – the dolphin and the dogfish. They swam near the surface, Cuckoo making beautiful leaps out of the water for air, Rock just swimming along steadily. It felt like a dream to Rock. He lost track of time completely. He was trying to concentrate on where they were swimming but his mind kept wandering. It turned out that Cuckoo was quite a music lover. He sang all the way. Rock couldn't understand the music of strange blips and bleeps, but he found it exhilarating none the less. He slipped into a strange euphoria, swimming along in time with Cuckoo's rhythmic melodies. Rock could have gone on like that for ever. But suddenly the water above them burst and Rock realised that they had company. It was Fargo the Albatross. Cuckoo stopped swimming.

'Hello, Fargo, old friend, how does the weather treat you?'

'I am happy that you have come, Cuckoo. Is there any way I can help you now on your mighty mission?'

'Well, I'm guessing that Orca and his family

are up north this time of year. Can you lead me to him?'

'It will be my pleasure, Cuckoo,' replied Fargo. 'Follow me.' And off they swam again. Fargo flew ahead and Cuckoo kept an eye on him whenever he had to leap for air.

Soon they lost track of time but Rock started to take note of his surroundings. The waters were colder, the scenery sparse. They passed many schools of fish dashing hither and thither; there was safety in numbers. A tension was building in the water. Everything moved faster and the atmosphere seemed rarer. There was almost no vegetation at all, only clear cold water – and fear. The sea was full of cold fear. Rock looked at Cuckoo. It was as impossible as ever to detect his true emotion. He was wearing his inscrutable dolphin mask: half-smile.

Suddenly Rock knew the whales were up ahead. He could hear them long before they came into view; they were playing near the surface and every now and then the water would pound against Rock's gills. He and Cuckoo swam towards them.

'Now I shall go,' announced Fargo.

'Thank you, my friend,' said Cuckoo. 'Now I owe you two.'

Two of what? thought Rock as Fargo beat the sea once with his wings and flew away. But Rock had no time for thinking. He and Cuckoo were being examined and probed by the curious whales.

'Don't react or show fear, whatever you do,' whispered Cuckoo. 'Just smile, or whistle or something. And keep close to me.'

Rock was bewildered. A baby whale, obviously inquisitive, stroked his belly with its own, and Rock laughed – he was ticklish. The whale mother thought this was most amusing.

Cuckoo was being addressed and challenged in Echo – dolphin and killer whale code – by all the whales he passed but all he would say was, 'Orca, Orca.'

Cuckoo led Rock right through the school of whales and up to the two most formidable looking creatures he had ever encountered. There suddenly seemed to be nothing but the whales. Everything was black and white. Even the water felt black and white. Rock looked behind him. The whales had formed a circle behind them. He looked up towards the surface – they were there too, floating on the surface and occasionally looking down through the water. They formed a huge dome above Rock and Cuckoo, and a huge mass below them: a multidimensional ring of killers.

Rock noticed that the whales' attention was on the two formidable creatures in front of them. He couldn't believe how cool and detached these creatures were. He could feel their minds, almost see the thoughts coming out of their giant brains, straining towards him and Cuckoo.

Finally Count Orca addressed Cuckoo. His voice was deep but gentle.

'Ah, my old friend Cuckoo Major, what a pleasure to see you again. This is my lady wife, Mary, Duchess of India.' Cuckoo bowed towards the lady.

'I am deeply honoured to meet the wife of my friend,' he replied.

Orca roared with laughter and the waters trembled and Mary, Duchess of India joined in too and then all the other whales. As the laughter gradually died down – Rock could not see the joke – Orca spoke:

'Why, Cuckoo, always the gallant gentleman. You remain true to form. But what have you brought with you? Not a gift for me, surely?' He beamed at Cuckoo. There was a twinkle in his eye. Rock felt nervous. He tried not to show it.

'I think,' said Cuckoo, 'that my small fishy friend here would be somewhat alarmed if he were handed over to you on a plate as a gift. He is only a humble dogfish, but I think you will agree he has shown great courage in coming here with me.'

'Oh, great courage, great courage,' agreed Orca, and started beating his huge flippers together in applause.

'Great courage, bravo,' agreed the other whales. They all started to beat their flippers as well. Rock thought he would suffocate with the pressure of the water on his gills. Cuckoo held him steady. The applause died down and there was a short silence when nobody spoke. It was Mary, Duchess of India who broke the silence.

'Either the dogfish has great courage or he is a fool.' Her voice was high-pitched and cold.

'My humble friend's name is Rock Salmon,' continued Cuckoo quickly before the other whales could start their choral accompaniment to the Duchess' remark. 'He and I have joined together with the main forces of Atlantis to combat a terrible threat to our way of life.

We are to be attacked by an evil enemy.

'An evil enemy?' muttered Orca. 'Who is this evil enemy?'

'Ernst Fishfinger,' replied Cuckoo, 'together with his army led by twenty fully trained Great White Sharks.'

There was another silence in the water. Then slowly and gradually the strange creatures started to beat their flippers again. Very slowly, like a slow hand-clap. And they started muttering to themselves under their breaths, very quietly. Rock was alarmed to say the least.

'Ernst Fishfinger,' replied Orca, backed by the rhythmic drumming of the other killer whales. 'Ernst Fishfinger. How fascinating. I know him well.' Rock could smell real danger in the water.

'Your move, my dear,' said Orca, turning towards Mary, Duchess of India. 'You will excuse us, Cuckoo, we are in the middle of a fascinating game of WHY with which your arrival coincided.'

'Of course, Count,' said Cuckoo diplomatically, looking at Rock out of one eye as though to hint not to be impatient. The other whales were still beating their flippers in time and chanting: 'Fishfinger, Fishfinger.' Count Orca and Mary Duchess of India were staring intently into one another's eyes as though they were engaged in some huge battle of will.

Suddenly Orca spoke. 'I know Fishfinger well. In fact he is right here with us now, at this very moment.'

'But that's impossible!' cried Rock, unable to contain himself.

'Silence!' bellowed Count Orca. Rock was trembling now. Cuckoo apologised to Orca on his behalf.

'Please excuse my small friend, Count. It is not unnatural that he should exhibit signs of alarm. He is after all very very small.'

Orca chuckled. The chuckle grew and exploded in an enormous guffaw. In the middle of the laugh, Rock observed that Fishfinger was indeed in their presence. He was on his disc drawn by his platoon of skates. He drew up by Orca's eye and stared right into it. Then he turned back, looked straight through Rock, and smiled that sickly gooey smile that Rock remembered so well.

'So good of you to be so understanding, Count,' said Fishfinger.

'My dear Fishfinger,' replied Orca, 'no problem, no problem at all.'

'And you will deal with these two and the girl?' inquired Fishfinger.

'Of course, right away,' replied the Count. Rock's mind was racing. *The girl. What girl?* His worst fears were soon confirmed. There she was, like a damsel in distress – Angel Sweetlips. She was clutching a strange shell in her fins towards which Fishfinger was directing his skates. The skates took it from her and Fishfinger and his retinue swam away.

'Angel, how did you get here?' cried Rock.

'Oh, Rock, I'm so frightened.'

At this point Cuckoo started screeching: 'What's going on? I don't understand. What's happening. Help! Help! Come on you two – swim for it.' There was a flurry of bubbles. All the whales seemed to be turned towards them.

'Why?' cried Rock. 'Why? All we wanted was some help. Why? Why?'

'Why, why, why, why?' chanted the whales, beating their flippers. 'Why, why, why?'

Count Orca burst out laughing again. 'Well done, Mary, my dear. What a brilliant move. I do believe you have won the game. 'WHY is so absorbing, don't you think?'

'Thank you, my dear,' replied Mary, Duchess

of India. 'You are such a gallant loser. Shall we have some lunch?'

'What a good idea. What's on the menu?'

'Angel, dogfish and dolphin sandwich, I think,' said Mary. 'A nice snack at least.'

'Yes,' replied Orca. 'Let's eat them . . . NOW.'

'Swim, swim, swim,' screeched Cuckoo. But it was no use. Angel and Rock were rooted to the spot. Rock felt his back being pushed and shoved and pulled about and he turned round and saw a huge row of gleaming white teeth bearing down towards him about to crunch into his flesh. He closed his eyes in panic . . .

'No, no.'

Then a voice:

'Wake up, Mr Salmon, wake up. You must have been having quite a nightmare.' Rock looked up. It was the friendly face of Sanderson. He looked around him. He was in Enzo Barracuda's office. No killer whales, no Cuckoo Major, no Fishfinger and no Angel Sweetlips. So at least there was still a chance that Cuckoo was having some joy with his mission to Count Orca. But Rock was incredibly relieved that he had not gone along with Cuckoo for the ride.

He was still frightened for Cuckoo's safety. After all, killer whales eat dolphins.

Rock rubbed his eyes and Sanderson presented him with a cup of coffee. The dream had been so vivid that he was still in a mild state of shock. Thank goodness reality could never be such a nightmare. *Or could it?* Rock shivered as he thought of Fishfinger.

11 · Memories

The rumour had spread. A full scale evacuation was under way. The city was gradually emptying. Schools of fish were scurrying out of their homes, leaving their belongings behind, concerned only with survival. *Who could blame them*, thought Rock, as he swam to Intergill. P.C. Dover escorted him to operations headquarters which had been hastily improvised. An anxious Hercule Poisson was busy over a map of Atlantis with Enzo Barracuda and Bluehop, the dolphin.

'Ah, Rock,' said Poisson, 'you've woken up at last. Feel better?'

'Much,' replied Rock. 'Give me the low-down.' He went over to the map.

'We've agreed between us that the army of Great Whites will operate to its least advantage within the confines of the city itself, so what they'll try to do is gradually to force us out into the open. We reckon we can hold them off for a certain amount of time. We've just got to pray that Cuckoo persuades Count Orca to come to our rescue. Meanwhile, we can send out detachments of shark patrols under the leadership of Hammerhead to make quick guerrilla attacks against individual Whites backed up by the dolphin patrol. Beside that there's not much we can do.'

'Cuckoo told us to suggest that Bluehop tries Man's net trick. Maybe that will help.'

'Yes, it will,' said Bluehop. 'But only for so long. The nets are being put into position at key points throughout the city at this very moment.'

'Good,' said Rock. 'One small point: where is the Sacred Chank?'

'It is quite safe, Mr Salmon,' said Enzo Barracuda quietly. 'I have deposited it in the vault of Otto Grass in Haddock Gardens.'

'And you're positive he is trustworthy?'

'Quite.'

'Now if there's nothing else, gentlemen, I suggest that we get to our various positions.'

'One question, if nobody objects, as it were?'

'Fire away, Sanderson,' said Rock.

'Who's organising the nets?'

'I've managed to persuade the Seahorse Union to do it,' said Bluehop. 'They're really fast. I've seen them rehearsing the manœuvre. They hook the ends of the net under their tails and then swim as fast as they can. Quite effective.'

'Thank you,' said Sanderson. 'Question answered.'

They all disbanded and went their separate ways. Rock felt rather useless. He was not sure what help he could be in the battle to come. However, he decided to check up on Otto Grass back in Haddock Gardens. He didn't trust him, and Enzo Barracuda had not put his mind at rest.

He could have saved himself the journey. When he arrived at the Prawnbroker's there was nobody around. The shutters were up. Rock decided it was not worth breaking in and snooping around because anything of interest was bound to be in Otto Grass' safekeeping. He wouldn't have left the chank. So Rock about-turned and swam back to where Bluehop and the seahorses were busy setting up nets. They were fearful devices. Bluehop was not looking his inscrutable self. His dolphin smile seemed to droop at the edges.

'What's on your mind, Bluehop?' asked Rock.

'It's these nets,' replied the dolphin. 'They bring back memories.' There was a moment of silence. Rock stared at Bluehop. His eyes seemed to grow sad as though mirroring some strange sense of suffering. He was staring blankly into empty water. Rock could see that his thoughts were miles away.

'These nets,' said Bluehop slowly, 'these nets of Man were and still are the cause of great misery to dolphins, and in fact to all Echo-speaking people.'

'They don't do fish much good either,' replied Rock, wistfully.

'Oh, of course, I know,' said Bluehop. 'But Man does not kill the dolphin for food. Perhaps I am being insensitive to your feelings, but I think you know what I mean. We kill to eat; you, a dogfish, kill to eat. It's not much of a consolation if you happen to be the unlucky fish that gets caught, but at least there's some sense behind it all. However, humans seem to have no sense. They enjoy murdering us with their nets.

'I remember once swimming in warm seas with Cuckoo and gradually feeling a terrible vibration growing in the water. And then the echoes began to reach us and we could not believe our radar. And then the smell of blood in the water and the horrific beating of panic-stricken flippers. There, up ahead, the sea was a mass of swirling foam, red with blood, sick with distress. There must have been four hundred dolphins caught in those vile Man nets, just like the ones we have here. Somehow or other Cuckoo and I managed to find reinforcements. The dolphin patrol are trained to deal with many kinds of emergencies.

'We managed somehow to break through the nets. It would have been a lot easier if the dolphins inside the nets had stayed still. None the less we saved nearly two hundred and fifty dolphins that day. I will never forget the sight of those other less fortunate dolphins that died. I will never swim near those waters again. Man is cruel.'

'Have you had any other experiences of Man?' asked Rock.

'Not personally,' replied Bluehop. 'But Cuckoo was once captured by Man. He understands human talk, you know.'

'I didn't know they could talk to each other,' said Rock in amazement.

'They can do many things that we cannot,' said Bluehop.

Rock laughed. 'They're so clumsy in the water.'

'Not so clumsy out of the water, though.'

'Yes, but there's nothing there, out of the water. Everyone knows that.'

'Don't be so sure, Rock,' replied Bluehop slowly. 'There is much to learn about Man.'

'You were telling me what happened to Cuckoo.'

'Oh yes. Cuckoo was once captured in a Man net, but they did not kill him. Instead they took him out of the water and travelled in a boat, far away. Cuckoo was frightened at first. But it soon became clear that these humans did not intend to harm him.

'They put him in a tiny sea surrounded by rock. He was alone there for many weeks. Soon he began to understand humans and realised that they were trying to learn the ways of the dolphins. Cuckoo was very lonely despite the fact that the humans tried hard to make friends with him. The only thought in his mind was how to escape. The small sea was right next to the ocean, but there seemed to be no way for him to be able to jump out into the sea and so

to freedom. Then one night he had an idea: he called all through the night as loudly as he could for his friend Fargo the Albatross. Fargo heard him and arrived next morning with twenty friends. In their beaks they each held a bit of Man-net. The escape was simple. They just flew over the tiny sea and Cuckoo leapt high out of the water and into the net. Before the humans could do anything the huge birds flew off and over the ocean and let go of the net and Cuckoo swam free. Cuckoo said that it was the happiest moment in his life, getting back into the ocean. And yet it is curious, is it not? The humans were always kind to him. Why were a handful of humans so kind to one dolphin, when others so willingly slaughter hundreds of dolphins in hot blood? Why?'

'I have no idea,' replied Rock. He was moved by Bluehop's story. 'Does Cuckoo's understanding of humans have anything to do with his apparent friendship with Count Orca, the killer whale?'

'Right first time,' said Bluehop. 'Cuckoo once heard humans talking on one of their boats. We dolphins love to swim alongside boats and have races with them. Anyway, Cuckoo overheard the humans saying that they were out to capture a baby killer whale in order to study it. He took it upon himself to warn Count Orca, who didn't believe him, but who none the less was sufficiently prudent to keep one eye open for any trouble. When the humans made their move towards one of the baby whales, Orca charged the boat and rammed it at top speed. The humans were not able to escape. Ever since then, Orca has acknowledged Cuckoo as a friend. That is a high honour,

because normally killer whales only regard dolphins as food.'

Rock was fascinated by the dolphin. He
started to tell him his strange dream about
Cuckoo and Count Orca and the game of
WHY?, but he did not get very far. A hum was
building in the water.

Was Rock about to enter into a reality worse
than any nightmare or fantasy? It would be true
to say at any rate that he was scared out of his
gills!

12 · The Dreaded Nets

The plan of action was perfectly simple. In Atlantis, apart from the different suburbs at various depths in the water, spreading over quite a large area, the real centre of the city consisted of one main street – Sundrown Strip – which was quite long and narrow and flanked by tall buildings on either side. The Great White Sharks would be bound to head down Sundrown Strip. They would find the city deserted and would gradually swim downtown to Okay Coral.

Bluehop had set up the nets at intervals along the main street. The Dolphin Patrol was at the ready to deal with any shark that happened to become entangled. The humming in the water was growing louder and louder. Rock and Bluehop looked at one another in an almost detatched way. Gone now was that sense of fear, replaced by an intense feeling of excitement. From here on it would be pure action. Rock peered out from behind his cover. He could now just about see them swimming into Sundrown Strip. They were led by Layla Blue, the slinky Blue Shark who had trained them so well. *Good*, thought Rock, *so far they're swimming straight towards the nets*. He ducked out of sight.

Closer and closer they came, until they were swimming right past Rock. He couldn't believe the size of the monsters. There was something uncanny about seeing them swim down such a narrow stretch of water. Bluehop allowed Layla Blue and two Great Whites through the first net, signalling to the seahorses to keep it well out of sight. Rock could see the gaping vicious faces of the sharks moving like flick-knives in slow motion from side to side.

Bluehop allowed Layla Blue through the second net too before he gave the signal to the seahorses on the first and second nets to swim up as fast as they could towards each other. The effect of this was incredible. Two Great Whites were trapped instantly in between the nets. The area was too narrow for the sharks behind to manœuvre in and to be of any direct assistance to them.

Meanwhile, the dolphins were charging at the two trapped sharks who were writhing around in the nets. Layla was shouting at them not to panic, to try to bite their way out calmly. But all her patient training and all her authority could not persuade the sharks to stay calm. Gradually, they started to suffocate, their gills trapped in the fine mesh. It was an awesome spectacle.

Layla managed to swim right over the nets with great presence of mind and ordered her forces to hold back for a while, until the two sharks floated to the surface.

There seemed to be a silence for a moment, as both sides watched the two dead monsters floating slowly upwards. Rock found it unnerving.

'Okay, men, you've just seen what happens when you're careless. Keep your eyes open for any more tricks like that!' Layla was in strict control of the sharks. Onwards they swam, like machines, with dead eyes and coarse skin and hideous rows of dog-like teeth. Rock wondered whether the big fish had been hypnotised to behave in such an orderly fashion. Unlikely for these death-machines evolved over millions of years to be able to function in a group.

The big question now was whether the dolphins would be able to trick another shark.

Bluehop tried his best. He let them all swim through the next net-position, and the next. There was no way they were going to be fooled. Now and then a shark would make a grab for a dolphin, and miss. The dolphin would leap to safety into one of the office buildings flanking The Strip. Luckily the windows and doorways were too large for Great Whites to enter. Rock assumed that Fishfinger would have brought an army of smaller fish to manœuvre in these confined spaces. But so far he had only spotted the big fish – apart from Layla Blue. Anyway, had Fishfinger's forces penetrated the buildings, they would have come up against Enzo Barracuda's Mob.

They all seemed to be playing a waiting game. The sharks were swimming painfully carefully and slowly. This suited Bluehop and Rock. After all, the idea was to stall for time until Cuckoo arrived with Count Orca. Rock noticed the last shark in the line lagging behind. He signalled this to Bluehop, who took immediate action and gave the sign to the seahorses. Within seconds, the shark was in the net. By the time the others had turned to help, it was all over.

Not bad, thought Rock. *Three sharks down.* But the surprise attack was too much even for Layla Blue, and Rock and Bluehop decided to take cover. The Great White Sharks started charging the buildings in their anger, to no avail. But it seemed certain that the net trick could not be used again.

'We ought to head off to Okay Coral,' whispered Bluehop. 'That's where we're to make our last swim.'

'That's also the rendezvous point for Cuckoo and Orca,' added Rock. 'How are we going to get there before them?'

'We'll just have to swim for it,' said Bluehop. 'If only we could delay them some more. It would make all the difference, I feel sure.'

The Great Whites were now snooping around carefully again. Layla had managed to cool their tempers. It was almost as if the sharks were waiting for the next move.

But nobody on either side was expecting what did happen next. The dolphins, Rock and the Mob forces were up ahead of the sharks who were swimming nearer and nearer to them. Bluehop was about to give the order to make a dash for it, when he heard the unmistakable sound of singing in the water.

'Rock, how could you sing at a time like this? You should be saving all your bubbles up for swimming.'

'It's not me, Bluehop,' said Rock breathlessly. 'I thought it was you.' It was neither of them. It seemed to be a quartet of male voices. They were singing a stirring song:

'*We're Carlos, Carlos, Carlos and Carlos*
  The Portuguese Men o' War;
The most gallant Armada loved in the hearts
  Of fish from shore to shore.'

Rock looked at Bluehop. Neither of them had ever heard of Carlos, Carlos, Carlos or Carlos. Rock almost seemed to shrug in disbelief. The singing was right overhead, between them and the enemy. Suddenly, Rock could no longer see the sharks. A kind of film was floating through the water between the two forces.

'Of course!' shouted Bluehop in great excitement. 'Portuguese Men o' War. They've provided us with our getaway. Come on! Let's not waste time. Off we go.'

And away they swam. As simple as that. The

sharks were once again taken by surprise. By the time the shimmering cloud had passed, the dolphins and the Mob were long gone.

Carlos, Carlos, Carlos and Carlos drifted off, singing their song. It was quite a while before Layla and her sharks were once again able to swim down Sundown Strip towards Okay Coral and their destiny. . . .

13 · Blood Over Atlantis

Poisson was already waiting for Bluehop and Rock. He was anxious.

'No sign of Cuckoo,' he announced gravely. 'We haven't got much time left.'

'You never can tell,' said Bluehop, philosophically.

Okay Coral was deserted except for them. Bluehop decided to form the dolphins into two lines, and they all waited in the water quite calmly for the enemy to arrive. Every now and then they would make for the surface, leap out of the water to take in air, and then dive down again.

The atmosphere was ghostly, or so it appeared to Rock. Perhaps it was because he knew that whether Orca arrived or not much blood would be spilt that day. Poisson did not have to say a word for Rock to realise that he was thinking exactly the same thing.

'How was it with the nets, Bluehop?'

'We managed to give them something to think about for a while. But they were very strong.'

'And Carlos, Carlos, Carlos and Carlos were a great help too,' added Rock. 'Where did they come from?'

'Ah,' exclaimed Poisson, 'the Portuguese Musketeers. I believe that they are old friends of Fargo the Albatross.'

The conversation was interrupted by the sounds of battle. Enzo Barracuda's Mob were obviously in close combat with the Whites. *Small chance they've got*, thought Rock. A huge cloud of blood started to rise above Atlantis. It was clearly visible from where Rock and the others had positioned themselves.

'Fishfinger is optimistic,' said Bluehop. 'We noticed earlier that he's only brought his army of Great Whites. If Orca does come to the rescue, we will certainly win the day.'

'If ... ' groaned Poisson. 'I wish I could be as optimistic as Monsieur Fishfinger.' Gradually the battle sounds died down. Rock had no way of knowing who was winning. He was so impatient to know, that he decided to swim in towards town a way.

He hadn't swum more than two-hundred yards when he heard voices.

'I'll get you, you crossed-eyed freak!' It was the voice of Ed Stingray. He was engaged in a deadly duel with Hammerhead. The two fish were circling one another.

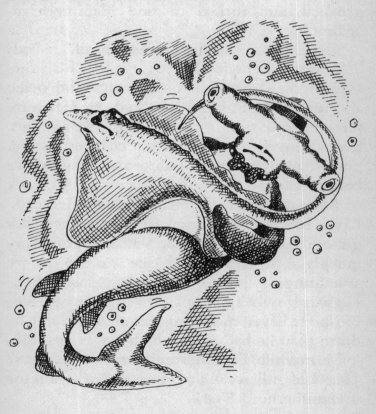

'Who's a pretty ray, then?' taunted Hammerhead.

This was more than Ed Stingray could bear. He swooped down towards Hammerhead, who easily sideswam him, turned, and gave him a vicious blow across the back. Stingray groaned, and turned to find Hammerhead again.

'Coochy-coo,' teased Hammerhead.

Stingray went for his foe again. This time Hammerhead decided to deal with him once and for all. As Stingray attacked, he met him full on and took him across the throat with his teeth. Stingray howled. Just at that moment a blue shape flew past Rock and straight at Hammerhead.

'My eye! My eye!' screamed Hammerhead. Layla Blue had appeared from nowhere and gone to Stingray's rescue. She disappeared as quickly as she had arrived. She was too late to save Stingray. His throat was in a sorry state. He was slowly spiralling towards the surface. He looked even more sinister and aggressive in death than he had in life, if that was possible.

Meanwhile, Hammerhead was in a bad way. He could only see out of one eye. Awkward for a Hammerhead Shark.

'Hey, Hammerhead, it's me, Rock Salmon. Are you okay?'

'Could be better, know what I mean, guv'?' replied Hammerhead. 'A bit tricky only having the use of one eye, like. Mind you, I suppose I could swim on my side and stick out my good eye dead ahead, get my drift?'

'Where's Barracuda?' asked Rock.

'Last time I saw him he said he was off looking for Fishfinger, guv'.'

'I hope he's okay.' Rock and Hammerhead swam to join Poisson and the others.

'Still no sign of Cuckoo,' muttered Poisson.

'Well,' said Bluehop. 'They're just about too late now anyhow. We've got company.' Rock Salmon froze.

14 · The Battle of Okay Coral

The Great White Sharks were quietly and slowly swimming towards Okay Coral. Bluehop and the Dolphin Patrol stayed in line, keeping as still as was dolphinly possible.

The sharks marched on until they were no more than twenty yards from the two lines of dolphins. Then they stopped.

'Squad, swim at ease,' shouted Layla Blue, who had successfully rejoined her team after her business with Hammerhead. The huge sharks started to swim in small circles. Sharks cannot stay still for one minute.

It was a strange sight: the impassive, inscrutable dolphins faced by a twitchy group of giant, organised killers. And not a killer whale in sight.

The atmosphere was electric. The waters of the sea were quite still, despite the ripples caused by the sharks as they silently turned in circles.

The dolphins were impassive: Rock and Poisson were in line behind them, Hammerhead was swimming in front of them – he had decided that his sideways swimming position did not suit the gravity of the situation and was swimming normally, even though he could only see out of one eye.

Next to the Great Whites, the normally dangerous-looking Hammerhead looked about as threatening as a Goldfish. Rock noticed that some of the Barracuda Mob had managed to escape from the battle with the Great Whites in one piece and were swimming along the bottom of the sea towards the small army that represented the last bastion of freedom for Atlantis.

No one uttered a word.

In the midst of the eerie silence there came a deep loud noise. It was the sound of a horn and it blasted through the water like a trumpet heralding the day of judgement. Everyone was straining their eyes to see where the noise had come from and what it meant. No one had the courage to swim towards the sound. Rock Salmon was frightened. Poisson did his best to try and reassure him, even though he was terrified as well.

Soon the horn sounded again, followed by another sound, the sound of Rollerfish – the skates that drew Fishfinger's disc. This sound was new to everyone except Rock, and he had to shout above the noise to tell them what it was. Fishfinger came into view, blowing his strange horn. Swimming close by and heavily guarded by two Great Whites was Enzo Barracuda.

'He must have fallen into a trap,' Rock shouted to Poisson.

'Yes, and that must be the Sacred Chank.'

'Of course!' cried Rock.

Fishfinger, with his retinue, swam up in front of his army and arrogantly inspected the troops, gloating over their obvious superiority.

It was quite clear that nothing was going to stop him conquering Atlantis now. All he had to do was give the word and the Great Whites, under Layla Blue, would move in swiftly for the kill.

Rock noticed that the waters had become dark, as though the sun did not want to witness the imminent slaughter.

Fishfinger had reached the last shark. The water seemed almost black.

'An excellent turn-out, Layla. You and the men are to be congratulated.'

Hammerhead at the head of the two lines of dolphins was seething with rage.

'Why don't you just get it over with, you fat creep,' he shouted at Fishfinger.

'Hold your tongue,' retorted Layla Blue.

'Come, come now,' replied Fishfinger in his most syrupy voice. 'All this is quite unnecessary, you know. I'm sure we can come to a very amicable arrangement and avoid bloodshed.'

'Fat chance,' mumbled Hammerhead.

'All I need is your guarantee that you will show allegiance to me,' went on Fishfinger, ignoring Hammerhead's remark. 'Life in Atlantis will go on. Of course there will be some minor changes. I will be in control and my army will protect you all from any further outside interference. So why don't we stop all of this mindless killing now.'

'Never,' cried Bluehop defiantly. 'I would rather die than live under the yoke of tyranny.'

'We'd rather cop our lot than fall in with the likes of you,' snarled Hammerhead.

'Bravo! bravo!' spoke a happy voice above them. Everyone looked up. It was Cuckoo Major.

Rock was dumbfounded. Cuckoo was back. Even more amazing – the water was dark not because the sun had disappeared but because there were twenty killer whales idly resting on the surface with their heads in the water, watching.

Fishfinger looked up in dismay. So did all the sharks.

Barracuda, who had been waiting his chance, now hurled himself at the unprepared Fish-finger. His charge managed to knock the over-weight fish clean off his disc, and he started plummetting downwards towards the sea bed. Barracuda didn't have a chance to chase him, for the Great White guard attacked him.

One of the killer whales lunged in to attack a shark, who swam for cover behind his com-rades.

Layla Blue realised that the only way out for her army was to fight. They were in deep water. She gave the signal and the Great Whites charged towards the surface.

'Killer Whales,' boomed a deep voice – Rock recognised it from his dream – it was Count Orca. 'Attack!'

All hell broke loose in the water. Rock Salmon and Poisson could only keep right out of the way and be spectators.

'This is better than going to the movies, sir, as it were,' spoke a small voice, as a killer whale tore into a Great White.

'Sanderson!' cried Rock, 'I'd forgotten all about you. Where have you been?'

'Right here with you all the time, sir. I've been as frightened as you.' They both watched as the battle got under way.

From the start it was clear that the odds were with the killer whales. Their initial attack dented any confidence the Great Whites had left and Orca marshalled his troops into a huge ring around the enemy.

The sharks couldn't attack everywhere at once. Whenever they made for one particular whale, the dolphin patrol, under Cuckoo and Bluehop, hurled themselves at the sharks with their deadly Frip Fu blows. And if any other White interfered, Orca soon sent another killer whale to deal with him.

It became quite clear why the killer whales were so called. The Whites were just beginning to despair when the whales changed tactics again. Five of them charged at the twelve remaining Whites. The Whites were brave. They fought well, using their vicious teeth to try to tear into the whales. But it was to no avail, for soon Orca sent in another five, then another. The beasts were so huge that the battle seemed to be in slow motion. Rock noticed out of the corner of his eye that Layla Blue was trying to slip away. He saw Enzo Barracuda swim off in pursuit. Hammerhead decided that the time had come for him to enter the fray. He gathered up his Mob and charged.

The battle was one-sided.

'The whales are almost playing with the sharks,' said Poisson, and Rock agreed. Count Orca neatly sideswam an attacker and turned, dealing him a lethal blow across the back with an enormous flipper. The whales were dancing through the battle, occasionally swimming to the surface for air. One crafty Great White thought he could use this to his advantage, as he trailed the whale to the surface. But his plan came to nothing when the whale leapt out of the water and came crashing back in right on top of him. Another whale was surprised by three sharks on his way to the surface. As they tore into him, he bellowed for help in Echo and two whales and a dolphin hurried to the rescue. The sharks fought like demons and Hammerhead threw himself into the battle too. Eventually, the sharks were beaten off but the whale was in bad shape as he limped away from the fight.

And so the battle raged for two hours with no mercy shown. And as the last of the Whites was dealt with, and the whales completely victorious, Rock saw the sun shining through the blood-drenched water. Count Orca's army swam to the surface to bask in the light and lick their wounds – these were mostly only slight, despite the fact that the sharks had fought for all they were worth. They had not managed to kill one single whale.

Count Orca was resting slightly apart from the rest of his whales. He was basking in the sun with his wife, who had fought as hard as anyone in the battle.

Cuckoo Major decided to take an official deputation up to Orca to thank him for saving the city. The deputation included Bluehop, Poisson, Rock Salmon, Hammerhead and Sanderson. Nobody had seen Enzo Barracuda since he had swam off to chase Layla Blue. They all moved towards the surface to express their gratitude to the leader of the whales. Cuckoo acted as spokesman:

'On behalf of everyone here and all the fish of Atlantis I would like to express my warmest thanks to you, my lord,' said Cuckoo meekly. There was a hint of sarcasm in his voice, as though he were being just a little too humble.

Orca turned towards Cuckoo, then back towards his wife. She started chuckling; and then Orca himself burst out laughing. The laughter was infectious. All the whales started joining in, beating the water with their flippers.

'Oh, Cuckoo, you tiny rogue,' sighed Orca. 'I dare say the time will come again when you will come to my aid. Your knowledge of Humans makes you quite unique you know. You're such an engaging little dolphin. I know that we killer whales are supposed to eat you, but I somehow think – and my wife Mary, Duchess of India, here agrees with me – I will always be glad to have you as a living friend rather than a dead lunch.'

All the dolphins started to laugh.

'Thank you, Count,' replied Cuckoo.

It has to be said the fish – Poisson, Rock, Sanderson and Hammerhead – were a little nervous of the killer whales. There was not one moment when Orca or any of the other whales as much as acknowledged their existence, let alone their presence. The favour had been done for

Cuckoo Major alone. The whales were completely indifferent to the fate of the city of Atlantis. Orca confirmed this:

'Cuckoo, my friend, I don't know why you bother with these fish. Why do you tie yourself down to them? You and your other dolphin friends should travel. You know there is far more to the ocean than Atlantis. You should go round the sea.'

'One day we will,' replied Cuckoo. 'But these people are my friends. I have respect for them.'

'Oh, well,' said Orca resignedly, 'it takes all sorts to make an ocean, I suppose.' With this he turned towards his wife and his colleagues the other whales.

'Well my friends, it's been quite an entertaining little afternoon, but I think it's time we were on our way.'

He turned back towards Cuckoo Major and looked him long in the eyes. There was a moment's silence, which Rock found very moving. The huge whale and the tiny dolphin were saying farewell. Then Cuckoo turned away, swam under the belly of Count Orca, touched his flipper with his own, and finally leapt up out of the water and skipped right over

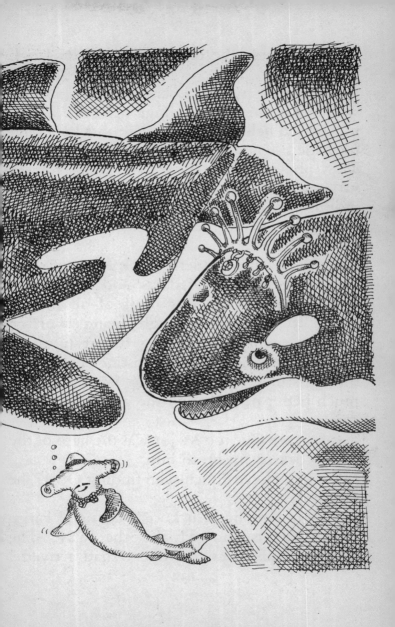

him. This made the other killer whales laugh again.

'Goodbye, my friend,' boomed Orca. 'Until we meet again.' As one huge mass the whales now dived below the surface almost knocking the little fish and the dolphins out of the way. They plunged deep, turned and made for the surface, leapt high in an arc and crashed back in unison. And away they swam.

Orca had saved the city.

After the whales had left, Rock felt a mixture of feelings – elation, sadness and exhaustion all rolled into one. But most of all he felt relief. It was bad enough being worried that the enemy were going to eat him up, even worse when it was a distinct possibility that his allies might do the same. He felt much better now that all the giants had gone away.

Of course Cuckoo Major was the hero of the day. Rock swam up to him.

'Did you have difficulty in finding Orca?' he asked.

'Oh, no,' replied Cuckoo. 'My friend Fargo the Albatross showed me the way. The strangest thing was that once I had arrived I

had to play a game with them called WHY?
Luckily I had my wits about me and won,
otherwise I don't think they'd have helped
me.'

Rock was longing to tell Cuckoo about his
dream, but he was interrupted by an excited
Hammerhead.

'Well I'll be fished!' said the one-eyed shark.

Rock turned round to see Enzo Barracuda
approaching with a prisoner. It was Layla Blue.
And he was also wearing the Sacred Chank tied
over his back with some seaweed.

'Fishfinger managed to escape,' said Barracuda, 'but we have a couple of mementos to
help us remember him.'

'Nice one, guv',' said Hammerhead.

There was only one more piece of excitement
at Okay Coral that day. Everyone was about
to leave the scene of the battle when the sea
went dark again. They all shivered and at once
were on their guard, each remembering the last
time that the waters had grown dark. They
looked upwards. There was no cause for alarm:
all the fish that had left Atlantis in flight before
the invasion had heard the good news and were
coming back. They looked nervous, but the

policeman in Inspector Poisson instinctively took over:

'It's all right. It's all over now. The danger is past. I'd like you all to go back to your homes now nice and quietly . . . That's it, no need to rush. Take your time.' Gradually they dispersed.

'Well, Inspector,' said Barracuda, 'I think it's time for me and my friends here to wish you a fond farewell. It was charming to swim along the straight and narrow with you. But all good things must come to an end.'

'It's a great pity that you don't operate on my side of the fence, Monsieur Barracuda,' said Poisson. 'You too, Hammerhead. Intergill could use fish like you.'

'Cor blimey,' replied the startled Hammerhead. 'I've been asked to help on many jobs in my time, but this is the first time anyone's ever offered me one as a copper.'

'You'd make a fine detective, Hammerhead,' joked Rock.

Everyone laughed.

'We'll stick to our line of work, if you don't mind, Inspector,' said Barracuda. 'The profits are better.'

Away they swam back to Atlantis. Poisson

was still singing their praises when Sanderson interrupted him.

'Er, excuse me, Inspector, but haven't you forgotten something, as it were?'

'Holy fish, Sanderson's right, Inspector!' exclaimed Rock. 'The Sacred Chank, Barracuda's swum off with the Chank!'

'Didn't you tell me, Rock, that it belonged to him in the first place?'

'Well, Angel Sweetlips was given it as a present.'

'If you ask me, he can keep the wretched thing. It's been about as important and valuable in this Fishfinger affair as the proverbial Red Herring.'

'As you wish, Inspector,' replied Rock. He was slightly annoyed about the Sacred Chank. But it was a small price to pay for the victory over the forces of evil.

'Come on, lads. Time for a drink at Ronnie's.'

'Good idea, Cuckoo,' replied Rock.

15 · Ronnie Scuba's Dive

Evening was sinking in the water and most of the celebrating had come to an end. It had really been party time down at *Ronnie Scuba's Dive*. The moment Cuckoo and the others swam in, it was drinks on the house. Rock must have told his adventures twenty times, each time becoming a little more elaborate in his account of the battle. Sanderson was surrounded by fellow pilot fish and toasted with drinks all night long. Eventually, everything began to quieten down. They were all growing tired. It had been a long day.

One by one the fish started saying goodnight and swimming home. Soon the only customers left were Cuckoo, Bluehop, Poisson, Rock and Sanderson. Sanderson was fast asleep attached to Rock.

They were all settled down in a comfortable corner of the bar listening to a band playing late-night cool jazz music. Bobby Guitar was on good form, and Joey Trumpet was playing the best little licks that Rock had ever heard him play.

Everyone felt mellow and relaxed. Rock was virtually slumped over the table. The band had gone into a smoochy version of *I've got you under my Fin*. Suddenly Rock sat up abruptly; Cuckoo was nudging him with his flipper.

'What's up, Cuckoo?'

'You've got a visitor, Rock.' He looked up.

'Mind if I join you, Rock?' It was Angel Sweetlips. She looked absolutely stunning in her fishnet dress and pearls and coral gill-rings.

Rock still did not know whose side Angel had played on in the Fishfinger/Stingray Saga.

'Be my guest, Angel,' replied Rock, cautiously. 'Sorry you lost your boyfriend.'

'Oh, you mean Ed? He had what was coming to him,' replied Angel. She passed that little test at any rate, thought Rock.

'Rock, I've got a small present for you, for the way you've put up with me and all the strange things that have happened. It's my way of saying thank you.'

With this, she put a bundle down on the

table. 'And now I'll leave you. You know how to get hold of me if you want me.'

Rock had his mouth open, but he was speechless – and Angel was gone.

'Well don't just sit there!' exclaimed Poisson. 'Open it.'

'But it might be a bomb. You can never tell with that lady,' replied Rock.

'Don't be daft,' said Bluehop and Cuckoo at the same time. 'Open the thing.'

After some persuading Rock agreed and slowly unwrapped the parcel. It was the Sacred Chank.

'That thing keeps turning up like a bad penny,' commented Poisson.

'Wait,' said Rock. 'There's a card.'

'What does it say?'

'Be patient . . .' Rock read the card to himself, then put it down on the table, got up and started to leave.

Poisson picked it up and read:

'Enzo returned this to me. I want you to have it. I've got an even better present for you . . . Love, Angel'.

'Trust Rock, *cherchez la femme*.' They all laughed.

Meanwhile, Rock was swimming along the

street outside *Ronnie's Dive* trying to catch up with Angel. The sea was very dark now. Visibility was bad. Suddenly he heard Angel's voice:

'Look out, Rock! Behind you.'

He turned around just in time to avoid a menacing tentacle clutching a stone. It was Otto Grass the Prawnbroker from Haddock Gardens.

'Damn you, Rock Salmon, you have wrecked all my plans,' he shrieked in a high-pitched voice.

'Otto, what a pleasant surprise,' replied Rock. 'So it's you who was behind everything. I knew there had to be one missing link.'

Otto made a lunge towards Rock, who managed to dodge him. But he swam right into another tentacle, and soon Otto had a tight grip round Rock's throat. The tentacles were covering his gills and he couldn't breathe. Luckily, Angel and Sanderson had rushed back to *Ronnie's* for help. Soon Cuckoo and Bluehop were on the scene.

Otto made a last-ditch effort to kill Rock and then let go with his ink sacs to try to make himself invisible. But he was no match for the artful dolphins. They soon had him cornered.

'Well, Rock,' said Bluehop, 'it looks like the lady here saved your skin.'

'Yes,' agreed Poisson. 'Now I think I will take this gentleman down to a nice quiet cell at Intergill Headquarters. Good night, my friends, sleep well.'

'Good night Inspector,' they all chorused.

Cuckoo said goodbye as well, did a couple of somersaults over Rock and Angel's heads, and swam off with Bluehop. They both leapt out of the water to take air.

'See you soon, Rock,' they called in Echo. Then they disappeared into the dark sea.

At last Rock was alone with Angel. It was a magic moment. He felt himself being drawn magnetically towards her. The last of the sun was sinking in the water. Rock closed his eyes.

Then out of the blue the spell was broken by a hiccup:

'Er, if you'll excuse me I don't think you'll be requiring my services any more tonight, sir, as it were.'

'Shrewd thinking, Sanderson,' was Rock's rather impatient reply.

'Well then, I'll say goodnight, sir, and Miss Sweetlips. Goodnight.'

'Sleep well, Sanderson,' said Angel. Sanderson swam away sheepishly.

The water felt good. The sea seemed to be in tune with itself. They could still hear the jazz playing down at *Ronnie's Dive*. Rock put his fin around Angel Sweetlips.

'Here's being hooked by you, kid,' he whispered to her.

They swam off together into the moonlight.

FIN

ANDREW DAVIES

Marmalade Atkins in Space

Most people think Marmalade Atkins is the worst-behaved girl in the world; Sister Purification and Sister Conception, who have to teach her think so; Cherith Ponsonby, headgirl of the Convent, thinks so; the staff of the El Poko Nightclub think so; even her parents think so!

Mrs Allgood, who is in the Helping Professions, knows the answer: Very Extreme Treatment. In VET, Bad Girls are sent off into space to be turned into Goody-Goodies. But has Mrs Allgood met her match in Marmalade?

Marmalade Atkins' Dreadful Deeds

Further hilarious adventures of a very bad girl. When Marmalade Atkins teams up with Rufus, the talking donkey who enjoys standing on people, her Dreadful Deeds become positively diabolical . . .!

Illustrated by John Laing

Based on the Thames Television series EDUCATING MARMALADE.

Thames/Magnet Books.